The American Diary of a Japanese Girl

Yoné Noguchi

The American Diary of a Japanese Girl

The present edition is a reproduction of previous publication of this classic work. Minor typographical errors may have been corrected without note; however, for an authentic reading experience the spelling, punctuation, and capitalization have been retained from the original text.

ISBN: 979-8-88830-422-8

To Her Majesty

HARUKO

Empress of Japan

January, 1902

Ever since my childhood, thy sovereign beauty has been all to me in benevolence and inspiration.

How often I watched thy august presence in happy amazement when thou didst pass along our Tokio streets! What a sad sensation I had all through me when thou wert just out of sight! If thou only knewest, I prayed, that I was one of thy daughters! I set it in my mind, a long time ago, that anything I did should be offered to our mother. How I wish I could say my own mother! Mother art thou, heavenly lady!

I am now going to publish my simple diary of my American journey.

And I humbly dedicate it unto thee, our beloved Empress, craving that thou wilt condescend to acknowledge that one of thy daughters had some charming hours even in a foreign land.

Morning Glory

BEFORE I SAILED

Tokio, Sept. 23rd

My new page of life is dawning.

A trip beyond the seas—Meriken Kenbutsu—it's not an ordinary event.

It is verily the first event in our family history that I could trace back for six centuries.

My to-day's dream of America—dream of a butterfly sipping on golden dews—was rudely broken by the artless chirrup of a hundred sparrows in my garden.

"Chui, chui! Chui, chui, chui!"

Bad sparrows!

My dream was silly but splendid.

Dream is no dream without silliness which is akin to poetry.

If my dream ever comes true!

24th—The song of gay children scattered over the street had subsided. The harvest moon shone like a yellow halo of "Nono Sama." All things in blessed Mitsuho No Kuni—the smallest ant also—bathed in sweet inspiring beams of beauty. The soft song that is not to be heard but to be felt, was in the air.

'Twas a crime, I judged, to squander lazily such a gracious graceful hour within doors.

I and my maid strolled to the Konpira shrine.

Her red stout fingers—like sweet potatoes—didn't appear so bad tonight, for the moon beautified every ugliness.

Our Emperor should proclaim forbidding woman to be out at any time except under the moonlight.

Without beauty woman is nothing. Face is the whole soul. I prefer death if I am not given a pair of dark velvety eyes.

What a shame even woman must grow old!

One stupid wrinkle on my face would be enough to stun me.

My pride is in my slim fingers of satin skin.

1

I'll carefully clean my roseate finger-nails before I'll land in America.

Our wooden clogs sounded melodious, like a rhythmic prayer unto the sky. Japs fit themselves to play music even with footgear. Every house with a lantern at its entrance looked a shrine cherishing a thousand idols within.

I kneeled to the Konpira god.

I didn't exactly see how to address him, being ignorant what sort of god he was.

I felt thirsty when I reached home. Before I pulled a bucket from the well, I peeped down into it. The moonbeams were beautifully stealing into the waters.

My tortoise-shell comb from my head dropped into the well.

The waters from far down smiled, heartily congratulating me on going to Amerikey.

25th—I thought all day long how I'll look in 'Merican dress.

26th—My shoes and six pairs of silk stockings arrived.

How I hoped they were Nippon silk!

One pair's value is 4 yens.

Extravagance! How dear!

I hardly see any bit of reason against bare feet.

Well, of course, it depends on how they are shaped.

A Japanese girl's feet are a sweet little piece. Their flatness and archlessness manifest their pathetic womanliness.

Feet tell as much as palms.

I have taken the same laborious care with my feet as with my hands. Now they have to retire into the heavy constrained shoes of America.

It's not so bad, however, to slip one's feet into gorgeous silk like that.

My shoes are of superior shape. They have a small high heel.

I'm glad they make me much taller.

A bamboo I set some three Summers ago cast its unusually melancholy shadow on the round paper window of my room, and whispered, "Sara! Sara! Sara!"

2

It sounded to me like a pallid voice of sayonara.

(By the way, the profuse tips of my bamboo are like the ostrich plumes of my new American hat.)

"Sayonara" never sounded before more sad, more thrilling.

My good-bye to "home sweet home" amid the camellias and white chrysanthemums is within ten days. The steamer "Belgic" leaves Yokohama on the sixth of next month. My beloved uncle is chaperon during my American journey.

27th—I scissored out the pictures from the 'Merican magazines.

(The magazines were all tired-looking back numbers. New ones are serviceable in their own home. Forgotten old actors stray into the villages for an inglorious tour. So it is with the magazines. Only the useless numbers come to Japan, I presume.)

The pictures—Meriken is a country of woman; that's why, I fancy, the pictures are chiefly of woman—showed me how to pick up the long skirt. That one act is the whole "business" of looking charming on the street. I apprehend that the grace of American ladies is in the serpentine curves of the figure, in the narrow waist.

Woman is the slave of beauty.

I applied my new corset to my body. I pulled it so hard.

It pained me.

28th—My heart was a lark.

I sang, but not in a trembling voice like a lark, some slices of school song.

I skipped around my garden.

Because it occurred to me finally that I'll appear beautiful in my new costume.

I smiled happily to the sunlight whose autumnal yellow flakes—how yellow they were!—fell upon my arm stretched to pluck a chrysanthemum.

I admit that my arm is brown.

But it's shapely.

29th—English of America—sir, it is light, unreserved and accessible—grew dear again. My love of it returned like the glow in a brazier that I had watched passionately, then left all the Summer days, and to which I turned my apologetic face with Winter's approaching steps.

Oya, oya, my book of Longfellow under the heavy coat of dust!

I dusted the book with care and veneration as I did a wee image of the Lord a month ago.

The same old gentle face of 'Merican poet—a poet need not always to sing, I assure you, of tragic lamentation and of "far-beyond"—stared at me from its frontispiece. I wondered if he ever dreamed his volume would be opened on the tiny brown palms of a Japan girl. A sudden fancy came to me as if he—the spirit of his picture—flung his critical impressive eyes at my elaborate cue with coral-headed pin, or upon my face.

Am I not a lovely young lady?

I had thrown Longfellow, many months ago, on the top shelf where a grave spider was encamping, and given every liberty to that reticent, studious, silver-haired gentleman Mr. Moth to tramp around the "Arcadie."

Mr. Moth ran out without giving his own "honourable" impression of the popular poet, when I let the pages flutter.

Large fatherly poet he is, but not unique. Uniqueness, however, has become commonplace.

Poet of "plain" plainness is he—plainness in thought and colour. Even his elegance is plain enough.

I must read Mr. Longfellow again as I used a year ago reclining in the Spring breeze,—"A Psalm of Life," "The Village Blacksmith," and half a dozen snatches from "Evangeline" or "The Song of Hiawatha" at the least. That is not because I am his devotee—I confess the poet of my taste isn't he—but only because he is a great idol of American ladies, as I am often told, and I may suffer the accusation of idiocy in America, if I be not charming enough to quote lines from his work.

30th—Many a year I have prayed for something more decent than a marriage offer.

I wonder if the generous destiny that will convey me to the illustrious country of "woman first" isn't the "something."

4

I am pleased to sail for Amerikey, being a woman.

Shall I have to become "naturalized" in America?

The Jap "gentleman"—who desires the old barbarity—persists still in fancying that girls are trading wares.

When he shall come to understand what is Love!

Fie on him!

I never felt more insulted than when I was asked in marriage by one unknown to me.

No Oriental man is qualified for civilisation, I declare.

Educate man, but—beg your pardon—not the woman!

Modern gyurls born in the enlightened period of Meiji are endowed with quite a remarkable soul.

I act as I choose. I haven't to wait for my mamma's approval to laugh when I incline to.

Oct. 1st—I stole into the looking-glass—woman loses almost her delight in life if without it—for the last glimpse of my hair in Japan style.

Butterfly mode!

I'll miss it adorning my small head, while I'm away from home.

I have often thought that Japanese display Oriental rhetoric—only oppressive rhetoric that palsies the spirit—in hair dressing. Its beauty isn't animation.

I longed for another new attraction on my head.

I felt sad, however, when I cut off all the paper cords from my hair.

I dreaded that the American method of dressing the hair might change my head into an absurd little thing.

My lengthy hair languished over my shoulders.

I laid me down on the bamboo porch in the pensive shape of a mermaid fresh from the sea.

The sportive breezes frolicked with my hair. They must be mischievous boys of the air.

I thought the reason why Meriken coiffure seemed savage and without art was mainly because it prized more of natural beauty.

Naturalness is the highest of all beauties.

Sayo shikaraba!

Let me learn the beauty of American freedom, starting with my hair!

Are you sure it's not slovenliness?

Woman's slovenliness is only forgiven where no gentleman is born.

2nd—Occasional forgetfulness, I venture to say, is one of woman's charms.

But I fear too many lapses in my case fill the background.

I amuse myself sometimes fancying whether I shall forget my husband's name (if I ever have one).

How shall I manage "shall" and "will"? My memory of it is faded.

I searched for a printed slip, "How to use Shall and Will." I pressed to explore even the pantry after it.

Afterward I recalled that Professor asserted that Americans were not precise in grammar. The affirmation of any professor isn't weighty enough. But my restlessness was cured somehow.

"This must be the age of Jap girls!" I ejaculated.

I was reading a paper on our bamboo land, penned by Mr. Somebody.

The style was inferior to Irving's.

I have read his gratifying "Sketch Book." I used to sleep holding it under my wooden pillow.

Woman feels happy to stretch her hand even in dream, and touch something that belongs to herself. "Sketch Book" was my child for many, many months.

Mr. Somebody has lavished adoring words over my sisters.

Arigato! Thank heavens!

If he didn't declare, however, that "no sensible musume will prefer a foreign raiment to her kimono!"

He failed to make of me a completely happy nightingale.

Shall I meet the Americans in our flapping gown?

I imagined myself hitting off a tune of "Karan Coron" with clogs, in circumspect steps, along Fifth Avenue of somewhere. The throng swarmed around me. They tugged my silken sleeves, which almost swept the ground, and inquired, "How much a yard?" Then they implored me to sing some Japanese ditty.

I'll not play any sensational rôle for any price.

Let me remain a homely lass, though I express no craft in Meriken dress.

Do I look shocking in a corset?

"In Pekin you have to speak Makey Hey Rah" is my belief.

3rd—My hand has seldom lifted anything weightier than a comb to adjust my hair flowing down my neck.

The "silver" knife (large and sharp enough to fight the Russians) dropped and cracked a bit of the rim of the big plate.

My hand tired.

My uncle and I were seated at a round table in a celebrated American restaurant, the "Western Sea House."

It was my first occasion to face an orderly heavy Meriken table d'hote.

Its fertile taste was oily, the oppressive smell emetic.

Must I make friends with it?

I am afraid my small stomach is only fitted for a bowl of rice and a few cuts of raw fish.

There is nothing more light, more inviting, than Japanese fare. It is like a sweet Summer villa with many a sliding shoji from which you smile into the breeze and sing to the stars.

Lightness is my choice.

When, I wondered, could I feel at home with American food!

My uncle is a Meriken "toow." He promised to show me a heap of things in America.

He is an 1884 Yale graduate. He occupies the marked seat of the chief secretary of the "Nippon Mining Company." He has procured leave for one year.

What were the questionable-looking fragments on the plate?

Pieces with pock-marks!

Cheese was their honourable name.

My uncle scared me by saying that some "charming" worms resided in them.

Pooh, pooh!

They emitted an annoying smell. You have to empty the choicest box of tooth powder after even the slightest intercourse with them.

I dare not make their acquaintance—no, not for a thousand yens.

I took a few of them in my pocket papers merely as a curiosity.

Shall I hang them on the door, so that the pest may not come near to our house?

(Even the pest-devils stay away from it, you see.)

4th—The "Belgic" makes one day's delay. She will leave on the seventh.

"Why not one week?" I cried.

I pray that I may sleep a few nights longer in my home. I grow sadder, thinking of my departure.

My mother shouldn't come to the Meriken wharf. Her tears may easily stop my American adventure.

I and my maid went to our Buddhist monastery.

I offered my good-bye to the graves of my grandparents. I decked them with elegant bunches of chrysanthemums.

When we turned our steps homeward the snowy-eyebrowed monk—how unearthly he appeared!—begged me not to forget my family's church while I am in America.

"Christians are barbarians. They eat beef at funerals," he said.

His voice was like a chant.

The winds brought a gush of melancholy evening prayer from the temple.

The tolling of the monastery bell was tragic.

"Goun! Goun! Goun!"

5th—A "chin koro" barked after me.

The Japanese little doggie doesn't know better. He has to encounter many a strange thing.

The tap of my shoes was a thrill to him. The rustling of my silk skirt—such a volatile sound—sounded an alarm to him.

I was hurrying along the road home from uncle's in Meriken dress.

What a new delight I felt to catch the peeping tips of my shoes from under my trailing koshi goromo.

I forced my skirt to wave, coveting a more satisfactory glance.

Did I look a suspicious character?

I was glad, it amused me to think the dog regarded me as a foreign girl.

Oh, how I wished to change me into a different style! Change is so pleasing.

My imitation was clever. It succeeded.

When I entered my house my maid was dismayed and said:

"Bikkuri shita! You terrified me. I took you for an ijin from Meriken country."

"Ho, ho! O ho, ho, ho!"

I passed gracefully (like a princess making her triumphant exit in the fifth act) into my chamber, leaving behind my happiest laughter and shut myself up.

I confess that I earned the most delicious moment I have had for a long time.

I cannot surrender under the accusation that Japs are only imitators, but I admit that we Nippon daughters are suited to be mimics.

Am I not gifted in the adroit art?

Where's Mr. Somebody who made himself useful to warn the musumes?

Then I began to rehearse the scene of my first interview with a white lady at San Francisco.

I opened Bartlett's English Conversation Book, and examined it to see if what I spoke was correct.

I sat on the writing table. Japanese houses set no chairs.

(Goodness, mottainai! I sat on the great book of Confucius.)

The mirror opposite me showed that I was a "little dear."

9

6th—It rained.

Soft, woolen Autumn rain like a gossamer!

Its suggestive sound is a far-away song which is half sob, half odor. The October rain is sweet sad poetry.

I slid open a paper door.

My house sits on the hill commanding a view over half Tokio and the Bay of Yedo.

My darling city—with an eternal tea and cake, with lanterns of festival—looked up to me through the gray veil of rain.

I felt as if Tokio were bidding me farewell.

Sayonara! My dear city!

ON THE OCEAN

"Belgic," 7th

Good night—native land!
Farewell, beloved Empress of Dai Nippon!

12th—The tossing spectacle of the waters (also the hostile smell of the ship) put my head in a whirl before the "Belgic" left the wharf.

The last five days have been a continuous nightmare. How many a time would I have preferred death!

My little self wholly exhausted by sea-sickness. Have I to drift to America in skin and bone?

I felt like a paper flag thrown in a tempest.

The human being is a ridiculously small piece. Nature plays with it and kills it when she pleases.

I cannot blame Balboa for his fancy, because he caught his first view from the peak in Darien.

It's not the "Pacific Ocean." The breaker of the world!

"Do you feel any better?" inquired my fellow passenger.

He is the new minister to the City of Mexico on his way to his post. My uncle is one of his closest friends.

What if Meriken ladies should mistake me for the "sweet" wife of such a shabby pock-marked gentleman?

It will be all right, I thought, for we shall part at San Francisco.

(The pock-mark is rare in America, Uncle said. No country has a special demand for it, I suppose.)

His boyish carelessness and samurai-fashioned courtesy are characteristic. His great laugh, "Ha, ha, ha!" echoes on half a mile.

He never leaves his wine glass alone. My uncle complains of his empty stomach.

The more the minister repeats his cup the more his eloquence rises on the Chinese question. He does not forget to keep up his honourable standard of diplomatist even in drinking, I fancy.

I see charm in the eloquence of a drunkard.

I exposed myself on deck for the first time.

I wasn't strong enough, alas! to face the threatening grandeur of the ocean. Its divineness struck and wounded me.

O such an expanse of oily-looking waters! O such a menacing largeness!

One star, just one sad star, shone above.

I thought that the little star was trembling alone on a deck of some ship in the sky.

Star and I cried.

13th—My first laughter on the ocean burst out while I was peeping at a label, "7 yens," inside the chimney-pot hat of our respected minister, when he was brushing it.

He must have bought that great headgear just on the eve of his appointment.

How stupid to leave such a bit of paper!

I laughed.

He asked what was so irresistibly funny.

I laughed more. I hardly repressed "My dear old man."

The "helpless me" clinging on the bed for many a day feels splendid to-day.

The ocean grew placid.

On the land my eyes meet with a thousand temptations. They are here opened for nothing but the waters or the sun-rays.

I don't gain any lesson, but I have learned to appreciate the demonstrations of light.

They were white. O what a heavenly whiteness!

The billows sang a grand slow song in blessing of the sun, sparkling their ivory teeth.

The voyage isn't bad, is it?

I planted myself on the open deck, facing Japan.

I am a mountain-worshipper.

Alas! I could not see that imperial dome of snow, Mount Fuji.

One dozen fairies—two dozen—roved down from the sky to the ocean.

I dreamed.

I was so very happy.

14th—What a confusion my hair has suffered! I haven't put it in order since I left the Orient. Such negligence of toilet would be fined by the police in Japan.

I was busy with my hair all the morning.

15th—The Sunday service was held.

There's nothing more natural on a voyage than to pray.

We have abandoned the land. The ocean has no bottom.

We die any moment "with bubbling groan, without a grave, unknelled, uncoffined, and unknown."

Only prayer makes us firm.

I addressed myself to the Great Invisible whose shadow lies across my heart.

He may not be the God of Christianity. He is not the Hotoke Sama of Buddhism.

Why don't those red-faced sailors hum heavenly-voiced hymns instead of—"swear?"

16th—Amerikey is away beyond.

Not even a speck of San Francisco in sight yet!

I amused myself thinking what would happen if I never returned home.

Marriage with a 'Merican, wealthy and comely?

I had well-nigh decided that I would not cross such an ocean again by ship. I would wait patiently until a trans-Pacific railroad is erected.

I was basking in the sun.

I fancied the "Belgic" navigating a wrong track.

What then?

Was I approaching lantern-eyed demons or howling cannibals?

"Iya, iya, no! I will proudly land on the historical island of Lotos Eaters." I said.

Why didn't I take Homer with me? The ocean is just the place for his majestic simplicity and lofty swing.

I recalled a few passages of "The Lotos Eaters" by Lord Tennyson—it sounds better than "the poet Tennyson." I love titles, but they are thought as common as millionaires nowadays.

A Jap poet has a different mode of speech.

Shall I pose as poet?

'Tis no great crime to do so.

I began my "Lotos Eaters" with the following mighty lines:

"O dreamy land of stealing shadows!
O peace-breathing land of calm afternoon!
O languid land of smile and lullaby!
O land of fragrant bliss and flower!
O eternal land of whispering Lotos Eaters!"

Then I feared that some impertinent poet might have said the same thing many a year before.

Poem manufacture is a slow job.

Modern people slight it, calling it an old fashion. Shall I give it up for some more brilliant up-to-date pose?

17th—I began to knit a gentleman's stockings in wool.

They will be a souvenir of this voyage.

(I cannot keep a secret.)

I tell you frankly that I designed them to be given to the gentleman who will be my future "beloved."

The wool is red, a symbol of my sanguine attachment.

The stockings cannot be much larger than my own feet. I dislike large-footed gentlemen.

18th—My uncle asked if my great work of poetical inspiration was completed.

"Uncle, I haven't written a dozen lines yet. My 'Lotos Eaters' is to be equal in length to 'The Lady of the Lake.' Now, see, Oji San, mine has to be far superior to the laureate's, not merely in quality, but in quantity as well. But I thought it was not the way of a sweet Japanese girl to plunder a garland from the old poet by writing in rivalry. Such a nice man Tennyson was!" I said.

14

I smiled and gazed on him slyly.

"So! You are very kind!" he jerked.

19th—I don't think San Francisco is very far off now. Shall I step out of the ship and walk?

Has the "Belgic" coal enough? I wonder how the sensible steamer can be so slow!

Let the blank pages pass quickly! Let me come face to face with the new chapter—"America!"

The gray monotone of life makes me insane.

Such an eternal absence of variety on the ocean!

20th—The moon—how large is the ocean moon!—sat above my head.

When I thought that that moon must have been visiting in my dearest home of Tokio, the tragic scene of my "Sayonara, mother!" instantly returned.

Tears on my cheeks!

Morning, 21st—Three P.M. of to-day!

At last!

Beautiful Miss Morning Glory shall land on her dream-land, Amerikey.

That's my humble name, sir.

18 years old.

(Why does the 'Merican lady regard it as an insult to be asked her own age?)

My knitting work wasn't half done. I look upon it as an omen that I shall have no luck in meeting with my husband.

Tsumaranai! What a barren life!

Our great minister was placing a button on his shirt. His trembling fingers were uncertain.

I snatched the shirt from his hand and exhibited my craft with the needle.

"I fancied that you modern girls were perfect strangers to the needle," he said.

15

He is not blockish, I thought, since he permits himself to employ irony.

My uncle was lamenting that he had not even one cigar left.

Both those gentlemen offered to help me in my dressing at the landing.

I declined gracefully.

Where is my looking-glass?

I must present myself very—very pretty.

IN AMERIKEY

San Francisco, night, 21ˢᵗ

"Good-bye, Mr. Belgic!"

I delight in personifying everything as a gentleman.

What does it mean under the sun! Kitsune ni tsukamareta wa! Evil fox, I suppose, got hold of me. "Gentlemen, is this real Amerikey?" I exclaimed.

Oya, ma, my Meriken dream was a complete failure.

Did I ever fancy any sky-invading dragon of smoke in my own America?

The smoke stifled me.

Why did I lock up my perfume bottle in my trunk?

I hardly endured the smell from the wagons at the wharf. Their rattling noise thrust itself into my head. A squad of Chinamen there puffed incessantly the menacing smell of cigars.

Were I the mayor of San Francisco—how romantic "the Mayor, Miss Morning Glory" sounds!—I would not pause a moment before erecting free bath-houses around the wharf.

I never dreamed that human beings could cast such an insulting smell.

The smell of honourable wagon drivers is the smell of a M-O-N-K-E-Y.

Their wild faces also prove their likeness to it.

They must have furnished all the evidence to Mr. Darwin. "The better part lies some distance from here," said my uncle.

I exclaimed how inhospitable the Americans were to receive visitors from the back door of the city.

We are not empty-stomached tramps rapping the kitchen door for a crust of bread.

We refused hotel carriage.

We walked from the Oriental wharf for the sake of the street sight-seeing.

17

Tamageta wa! A house was whirling along the street. Look at the horseless car! How could it be possible to pull it with a rope under ground!

Everything reveals a huge scale of measurement.

The continental spectacle is different from that of our islands.

We 40,000,000 Japs must raise our heads from wee bits of land. There's no room to stretch elbows. We have to stay like dwarf trees.

I shouldn't be surprised if the Americans exclaim in Japan, "What a petty show!"

Such a riotous rush! What a deafening uproar!

The lazy halt of a moment on the street must have been regarded, I fancied, as a violation of the law.

I wondered whether one dozen were not slain each hour on Market Street by the cars.

Cars! Cars! And cars!

It was no use to look beautiful in such a cyclone city. Not even one gentleman moved his admiring eyes to my face.

How sad!

I thought it must be some festival.

"No, the usual Saturday throng!" my uncle said.

Then I asked myself whether Tokio streets were only like a midnight of this city.

My beloved minister kept his mouth open—what heavy lips he had!—amazed at the high edifices.

"O ho, that's astonishing!" he cried, throwing his sottish eyes on the clock of the Chronicle building.

"Boys are commenting on you," I whispered.

I beseeched him not to act so droll.

He tossed out in his careless fashion his everlasting heroic laughter, "Ha, ha, ha——"

A hawkish lad—I have not seen one sleepy fellow yet—drew near the minister shortly after we left the wharf, and begged to carry his bag.

He was only too glad to be assisted. The brown diplomatist thought it a loving deed toward a foreigner.

He bowed after some blocks, thanking the boy with a hearty "arigato."

18

"Sir, you have to pay me two bits!"

His hand went to his pocket, when my uncle tapped his stooping back, speaking: "This is the country of eternal 'pay, pay, pay,' old man!"

"What does a genuine American beggar look like?" was my old question.

The Meriken beggar my friend saw at Yokohama park was dressed up in a swallow-tail coat. Emerson's essays were in his hand. He was such a genteel Mr. Beggar, she said.

I often heard that everybody is a millionaire in America. I thought it likely that I should see a swell Mr. Beggar among the Americans.

How many a time had I planned to make a special trip to Yokohama for acquaintance with the honourable Emerson scholar!

Alas, it was merely a fancy!

I have seen Mr. Beggar on the street.

He didn't appear in the formal dignity of a dress coat.

Where was his Emerson?

He was not unlike his Oriental brothers, after all.

He stood, because he wasn't used to kneeling like the Japs.

The only difference was that he carried pencils instead of a musical instrument.

He is a merchant,—this is a business country,—while the Japanese Mr. Beggar is an artist, I suppose.

My little gold watch pointed eleven.

I have been writing for some hours about my first impression of the city from the wharf, and my journey from there to this Palace Hotel.

The number of my room is 489.

I fear I may not return if I once go out. It's so hard to remember the number.

The large mirror reflected me as being so very small in the big room.

Such a great room with high ceiling!

I don't feel at home at all.

Not a petal of flower. No inviting picture on the wall!

I was tired of hearing the artificial greeting, "Irasshai mashi," or "Honourable welcome," of the eternally bowing Japanese hotel attendants.

But the too simple treatment of 'Merican hotel is hardly to my taste.

Not even one girl to wait on me here!

No "honourable tea and cake."

22nd—I need repose. The last few weeks have stirred me dreadfully. I will slumber just comfortably day after day, I decided.

But the same feeling as on the ocean returned.

My American bed acted like water, waving at even my slightest motion.

I fancied I was exercising even in sleep.

It is too soft.

Nothing can put me at complete ease like my hereditary lying on the floor.

I was restless all the night long.

I got up, since the bed was no joy.

Oh, the blue sky!

I thought I should never again see a sapphire sky while I am here. I was wrong.

This is church day.

The bells of the street-cars sounded musical.

The sky appeared in best Sunday dress.

I felt happy thinking that I should see the stars from my hotel window to-night.

I made many useless trips up and down the elevator for fun.

What a tickling dizziness I tasted!

I close my eyes when it goes.

It's an awfully new thing, I reckon.

Something on the same plan, I imagine, as a "seriage" of the Japanese stage for a footless ghost rising to vanish.

It is astonishing to notice what a condescending manner the white gentlemen display toward ladies.

They take off their hats in the elevator—some showing such a great bald head, like a funny O Binzuru, that is as common as spectacled children—if any woman is present. They stand humbly as Japs to the august "Son of Heaven." They crawl out like lambs after the woman steps away.

It puzzles me to solve how women can be deserving of such honour.

What a goody-goody act!

But I wonder how they behave themselves before God!

23rd—It is delightful to sit opposite the whitest of linen and—to portray on it the face of an imaginary Mr. Sweetheart while eating.

Whiteness is appetising.

And the boldly-marked creases of the linen are so dear. Without them the linen is not half so inviting.

I was taught the beauty of single line in drawing class some years ago.

But now for the first time I fully comprehended it from the Meriken tablecloth.

I wished I could ever stay gazing at it.

If I start my housekeeping in this country—do I ever dream of it?—I shall not hesitate to invest all my money in linen.

I laughed when I fancied that I sat with my husband—where's he in the world?—spreading a skilfully ironed linen cloth on the Spring grasses (what a gratifying white and green!), and I upset a teapot over the linen, while he ran after water;—then I picked all the buttercups and covered the dark red stain.

The minister makes a ridiculous show of himself in the dining-room.

His laughter draws the attention of every lady.

This morning he exclaimed: "Americans have no courtesy for strangers, except meaning money."

And he finished his speech with his boisterous "Ha, ha, ha!"

A pale impatient lady, like a trembling winter leaf, sitting at the table next to us, shrugged her shoulders and muttered, "Oh, my!"

21

I hoped I could invent any scheme to make him hasten to his post—Kara or Tenjiku, whatever place it be.

He is good-natured like a rubber stamp.

But I am sorry to say that he does not fit Amerikey.

I was relieved when he announced that his departure would occur to-morrow.

My dignity was saved.

I cut a square piece of paper. I pencilled on it as follows:

> To the Japanese Legation.
> The City of Mexico.
> Handle Carefully, Easily Broken.

I put it on the large palm of the minister. I warned him that he should never forget to pin it on his breast.

"Mean little thing you are!" he said.

And his great happy "Ha, ha, ha!" followed as usual.

Bye-bye!

The negroes are horrid. I scanned them on the first chance of my life.

What is the standard of beauty of their tribe, I am eager to be informed!

I searched for "coon" in my dictionary. The explanation was unsatisfactory.

The ever-so-kind Americans don't consider them, I am certain, as "animals allied to the bear."

Tell me what it means.

24th—Spittoon!

The American spittoon is famous, Uncle says.

From every corner in this nine-story hotel—think of its eight hundred and fifty-one rooms!—you are met by the greeting of the spittoon.

How many thousand are there?

It must be a tremendous task to keep them clean as they are.

I wonder why the proprietor doesn't give the city the benefit of some of them.

San Francisco ought to place spittoons along the sidewalk.

The ladies wear such a long gaudy skirt.

And it is quite a fashion of modern gents, it appears, to spit on the pavements.

This Palace Hotel is a palace.

You drop into the toilet room, for instance.

You cannot help exclaiming: "Iya, haya, Japan is three centuries behind!"

Everything presents to you a silent lecture of scientific modernism.

Whenever I am bothered too much by my uncle I lock myself up in the toilet room. There I feel the whole world is mine.

I can take off my shoes. I can play acrobat if I prefer.

Nobody can spy me.

It is the place where you can pray or cry all you desire without one interruption.

My room is great, equipped with every new invention. Numbers of electric globes dazzle with kingly light above my head.

If I enter my room at dusk, I push a button of electricity.

What a satisfaction I earn seeing every light appear to my honourable service!

I look upon my finger wondering how such an Oriental little thing can make itself potent like the mighty thumb of Mr. Edison.

25th—What a novel sensation I felt in writing "San Francisco, U.S.A.," at the head of my tablet!

(What agitation I shall feel when I write my first "Mrs." before my name! Woman must grow tired of being addressed "Miss," sooner or later.)

I have often said that I hardly saw any necessity for corresponding when one lives on such a small island as Japan.

I could see my friends in a day or two, at whatever place I was.

I have now the ocean between me and my home.

Letter writing is worth while.

I did not know it was such a sweet piece of work.

I should declare it to be as legitimate and inexpensive a game as ever woman could indulge in.

I was stepping along the courtyard of this hotel.

I have seen a gentleman kissing a woman.

I felt my face catching fire.

Is it not a shame in a public place?

I returned to my apartment. The mirror showed my cheeks still blushing.

The Japanese consul and his Meriken wife—she is some inches higher than her darling—paid us a call.

I said to myself that they did not match well. It was like a hired haori with a different coat of arms.

The Consul looked proud, as if he carried a crocodile.

Mrs. Consul invited us for luncheon next Sunday.

"Quite a family party—O ho, ho!"

Her voice was unceremonious.

I noticed that one of her hairpins was about to drop. I thought that Meriken woman was as careless as I.

How many hairpins do you suppose I lost yesterday?

Four! Isn't that awful?

My uncle innocently stated to her I was a great belle of Tokio.

I secretly pinched his arm through his coat-sleeve. My little signal did not influence him at all. He kept on his hyperbolical advertisement of me.

She promised a beautiful girl to meet me on Sunday.

I fancied how she looked.

I thought my performance of the first interview with Meriken woman was excellent. But my rehearsal at home was useless.

26th—I lost my little charm.

It worried me awfully.

It was given me by my old-fashioned mother. She got it after a holy journey of one month to the shrine of Tenno Sama.

I should be safe, Mother said, from water, fire and

highwayman (what else, God only knows) as long as I should carry it.

I sought after it everywhere. I begged my uncle to let me examine his trunk.

"Cast off an ancient superstition!" Uncle scorned.

I sat languidly on the large armchair which almost swallowed my small body.

I imagined many a punishment already inflicted on me.

The tick-tack of my watch from my waist encouraged my nervousness.

There is nothing more irritating than a tick-tack.

I locked up my watch in the drawer of the dresser.

I still felt its tick-tack pursuing my ears.

Then I put it under the pillow.

27th—How I wished I could exchange a ten-dollar gold-piece for a tassel of curly hair!

American woman is nothing without it.

Its infirm gesticulation is a temptation.

In Japan I regarded it as bad luck to own waving hair.

But my tastes cannot remain unaltered in Amerikey.

I don't mind being covered with even red hair.

Red hair is vivacity, fit for Summer's shiny air.

I remember that I trembled at sight of the red hair of an American woman at Tokio. Japanese regard it as the hair of the red demon in Jigoku.

I sat before the looking-glass, with a pair of curling-tongs.

I tried to manage them with surprising patience. I assure you God doesn't vouchsafe me much patience.

Such disobedient tools!

They didn't work at all. I threw them on the floor in indignation.

My wrists pained.

I sat on the floor, stretching out my legs. My shoe-strings were loosed, but my hand did not hasten to them.

I was exhausted with making my hair curl.

I sent my uncle to fetch a hair-dresser.

28th—How old is she?

I could never suggest the age of a Meriken woman.

That Miss Ada was a beauty.

It's becoming clearer to me now why California puts so much pride in her own girls.

Ada was a San Franciscan whom Mrs. Consul presented to me.

What was her family name?

Never mind! It is an extra to remember it for girls. We don't use it.

How envious I was of her long eyelashes lacing around the large eyes of brown hue!

Brown was my preference for the velvet hanao of my wooden clogs.

Long eyelashes are a grace, like the long skirt.

I know that she is a clever young thing.

She was learned in the art of raising and dropping her curtain of eyelashes. That is the art of being enchanting. I had said that nothing could beat the beauty of my black eyes. But I see there are other pretty eyes in this world.

Everything doesn't grow in Japan. Noses particularly.

My sweet Ada's nose was an inspiration, like the snow-capped peak of O Fuji San. It rose calmly—how symmetrically!—from between her eyebrows.

I had thought that 'Merican nose was rugged, big of bone.

I see an exception in Ada.

She must be the pattern of Meriken beauty.

I felt that I was so very homely.

I stole a sly glance into the looking-glass, and convinced myself that I was a beauty also, but Oriental.

We had different attractions.

She may be Spring white sunshine, while I am yellow Autumn moonbeams. One is animation, and the other sweetness.

I smiled.

She smiled back promptly.

We promised love in our little smile.

She placed her hand on my shoulder. How her diamond ring flashed! She praised the satin skin of my face.

She was very white, with a few sprinkles of freckles. Their scattering added briskness to the face in her case. (But doesn't San Francisco produce too many freckles in woman?) The texture of Ada's skin wasn't fine. Her face was like a ripe peach with powdery hair.

Is it true that dark skin is gaining popularity in American society?

The Japanese type of beauty is coming to the front then, I am happy.

I repaid her compliment, praising her elegant set of teeth.

Ada is the free-born girl of modern Amerikey.

She need never fear to open her mouth wide.

She must have been using special tooth-powder three times a day.

"We are great friends already, aren't we?" I said.

And I extended my finger-tips behind her, and pulled some wisps of her chestnut hair.

"Please, don't!" she said, and raised her sweetly accusing eyes. Then our friendship was confirmed.

Girls don't take much time to exchange their faith.

I was uneasy at first, thinking that Ada might settle herself in a tête-à-tête with me, in the chit-chat of poetry. I tried to recollect how the first line of the "Psalm of Life" went, for Longfellow would of course be the first one to encounter.

Alas, I had forgotten it all.

I was glad that her query did not roam from the remote corner of poesy.

"Do you play golf?" she asked.

She thinks the same things are going on in Japan.

Ada! Poor Ada!

The honourable consul and my uncle looked stupid at the lunch table.

I thought they were afraid of being given some difficult question by the Meriken ladies.

Mrs. Consul and Ada ate like hungry pigs. (I beg their pardon!)

"You eat like a pussy!" is no adequate compliment to pay to a Meriken woman.

I found out that their English was neither Macaulay's nor Irving's.

29th—I ate a tongue and some ox-tail soup.

Think of a suspicious spumy tongue and that dirty bamboo tail!

Isn't it shocking to even incline to taste them?

My mother would not permit me to step into the holy ground of any shrine in Japan. She would declare me perfectly defiled by such food.

I shall turn into a beast in the jungle by and by, I should say.

My uncle committed a greater indecency. He ate a tripe.

It was cooked in the "western sea egg-plant," to taste of which brings on the small-pox, as I have been told.

He said that he took a delight in pig's feet.

Shame on the Nippon gentleman!

Harai tamae! Kiyome tamae!

30th—"Chui, chui, chui!"

A little sparrow was twittering at my hotel window.

I could not believe that the sparrow of large America could be as small as the Nippon-born.

Horses are large here. Woman's mouth is large, something like that of an alligator. Policeman is too large.

I fancied that little birdie might be one strayed from the bamboo bush of my family's monastery.

"Sweet vagabond, did you cross the ocean for Meriken Kenbutsu?" I said.

"Chui, chui! Chui, chui, chui!" he chirped.

Is "chui, chui" English, I wonder?

I pushed the window up to receive him.

Oya, ma, he has gone!

I felt so sorry.

I was yearning after my beloved home.

This is the great Chrysanthemum season at home. I missed the show at Dangozaka.

How gracefully the time used to pass in Dai Nippon, while I sat looking at the flowers on a tokonoma.

Every place is a strange gray waste to me without the intimate faces of flowers.

Flowers have no price in Japan, just as a poet is nothing, for everybody there is poet. But they have a big value in this city— although I am not positive that an American poet creates wealth.

I purchased a select bouquet of violets.

I passed by several young gentlemen. Were their eyes set on my flowers or my hands?

I don't wear gloves. I don't wish my hands to be touched harshly by them. Truly I am vain of showing my small hands.

I love the violet, because it was the favorite of dear John— Keats, of course.

It may not be a flower. It is decidedly a perfume, anyhow.

31st—I have heard a sad piece of news from Mrs. Consul about Mr. Longfellow.

She says that he has ceased to be an idol of American ladies.

He has retired to a comfortable fireside to take care of school children.

Poor old poet!

Nov. 1st—American chair is too high.

Are my legs too short?

It was uncomfortable to sit erect on a chair all the time as if one were being presented before the judge.

And those corsets and shoes!

They seized me mercilessly.

I said that I would spend a few hours in Japan style, reclining on the floor like an eloped angel.

I brought out a crape kimono and my girdle with the phœnix embroidery, after having locked the entrance of my room.

"Kotsu, kotsu, kotsu!"

Somebody was fisting on my door.

Oya, she was Ada, my "Rose of Frisco" or "Butterfly of Van Ness."

(She was quartered in Van Ness Avenue, the most elegant street of a whole bunch.)

She was sprightly as a runaway princess. She blew her sunlight and fragrance into my face.

I was grateful that I chanced to be acquainted with such a delightful Meriken lady.

"O ho, Japanese kimono! If I might only try it on!" she said.

I told her she could.

"How lovely!" she ejaculated.

We promised to spend a gala day together.

"We will rehearse," I said, "a one-act Japanese play entitled 'Two Cherry Blossom Musumes.'"

I assisted her to dress up. She was utterly ignorant of Oriental attire.

What a superb development she had in body! Her chest was abundant, her shoulders gracefully commanding. Her rather large rump, however, did not show to advantage in waving dress. Japs prefer a small one.

My physical state is in poverty.

I was wrong to believe that the beauty of woman is in her face.

It is so, of course, in Japan. The brown woman eternally sits. The face is her complete exhibition.

The beauty of Meriken woman is in her shape.

I pray that my body may grow.

The Japanese theatre never begins without three rappings of time-honoured wooden blocks.

I knocked on the pitcher.

Miss Ada appeared from the dressing room, fluttering an open fan.

How ridiculously she stepped!

It was the way Miss What's-her-name acted in "The Geisha," she said.

She was much taller than little me. The kimono scarcely reached to her shoes. I have never seen such an absurd show in my life.

30

I was tittering.

The charming Ada fanned and giggled incessantly in supposed-to-be Japanese chic.

"What have I to say, Morning Glory?" she said, looking up.

"I don't know, dear girl!" I jerked.

Then we both laughed.

Ada caught my neck by her arm. She squandered her kisses on me.

(It was my first taste of the kiss.)

We two young ladies in wanton garments rolled down happily on the floor.

2nd—If I could be a gentleman for just one day!

I would rest myself on the hospitable chair of a barber shop—barber shop, drug store and candy store are three beauties on the street—like a prince of leisure, and dream something great, while the man is busy with a razor.

I am envious of the gentleman who may bathe in such a purple hour.

I never rest.

American ladies neither!

Each one of them looks worried as if she expected the door-bell any moment.

I suppose it is the penalty of being a woman.

3rd—My little heart was flooded with patriotism.

It is our Mikado's birthday.

I sang "The Age of Our Sovereign." I shouted "Ten thousand years! Banzai! Ban banzai!"

My uncle and I hurried to the Japanese Consulate to celebrate this grand day.

4th—The gentlemen of San Francisco are gallant.

They never permit the ladies—even a black servant is in the honourable list of "ladies"—to stand in the car.

If Oriental gentlemen could demean themselves like that for just one day!

I should not mind a bit if one proposed to me even.

I love a handsome face.

They part their hair in the middle. They have inherited no bad habit of biting their finger-nails. I suppose they offer a grace before each meal. Their smile isn't sardonic, and their laughter is open.

I have no dispute with their mustaches and their blue eyes. But I am far from being an admirer of their red faces.

Japs are pygmies. I fear that the Americans are too tall. My future husband is not allowed to be over five feet five inches. His nose should be of the cast of Robert Stevenson's.

Each one of them carries a high look. He may be the President at the next election, he seems to say. How mean that only one head is in demand!

A directory and a dictionary are kind. The 'Merican husband is like them, I imagine.

I have no gentleman friend yet.

To pace alone on the street is a melancholy discarded sight.

What do you do if your shoe-string comes untied?

I have seen a gentleman fingering the shoestrings of a lady. How glad he was to serve again, when she said, "That's too tight!"

Shall my uncle fill such a part?

Poor uncle!

Old company, however, isn't style.

He is forty-five.

Why can I not choose one to hire from among the "bully" young men loitering around a cigar-stand?

5th—My uncle was going out in a black frock-coat and tea-coloured trousers. I insisted that his coat and trousers didn't match.

How can a man be so ridiculous?

I declared that it was as poor taste as for a darkey to wear a red ribbon in her smoky hair.

Uncle surrendered.

He said, "Hei, hei, hei!"

Goo' boy!

He dismissed the great tea-colour.

6th—We had a shower.

The city dipped in a bath.

The pedestrians threw their vaguely delicate shadows on the pavements. The ladies voluntarily permitted the gentlemen to review their legs. If I were in command, I would not permit the ladies to raise an umbrella under the "para para" of a shower. Their hastening figures are so fascinating.

The shower stopped. The pavements were glossed like a looking-glass. The windows facing the sun scattered their sparkling laughter.

How beautiful!

I am perfectly delighted by this city.

One thing that disappoints me, however, is that Frisco is eternally snowless,

Without snow the year is incomplete, like a departure without sayonara.

Dear snow! O Yuki San!

Many Winters ago I modelled a doll of snow, which was supposed to be a gentleman.

How proud I used to be when I stamped the first mark with my high ashida on the white ground before anyone else!

I wonder how Santa Claus will array himself to call on this town.

His fur coat is not appropriate at all.

7th—Why didn't I come to Amerikey earlier—in the Summer season?

I was staring sadly at my purple parasol against the wall by my dresser.

I have no chance to show it.

I have often been told that I look so beautiful under it.

8th—My darling O Ada came in a carriage. Her two-horsed carriage was like that of our Japanese premier.

She is the daughter of a banker.

The sun shone in yellow.

Ada's complexion added a brilliancy. I was shocked, fearing that I looked awfully brown.

Ada said that I was "perfectly lovely." Can I trust a woman's eulogy?

I myself often use flattery.

A jewel and face-powder were not the only things, I said, essential to woman.

We drove to the Golden Gate Park and then to the Cliff House.

What a triumphant sound the hoofs of the bay horses struck! I fancied the horses were a poet, they were rhyming.

I don't like the automobile.

Ada was sweet as could be.

"Tell me your honourable love story!" she chattered.

I did only blush.

I hadn't the courage to burst my secrecy.

I loved once truly.

It was an innocent love as from a fairy book.

If true love could be realised!

In the park I noticed a lady who scissored the "don't touch" flowers and stepped away with a saintly air. The comical fancy came to me that she was the mother of a policeman guarding against intruders.

We found ourselves in the Japanese tea garden.

A tiny musume in wooden clogs brought us an honourable tea and o'senbe.

The grounds were an imitation of Japanese landscape gardening.

Homesickness ran through my fibre.

The decorative bridge, a stork by the brook, and the dwarf plants hinted to me of my home garden.

A sudden vibration of shamisen was flung from the Japanese cottage close by.

"Tenu, tenu! Tenu, tsunn shann!"

Who was the player?

When I sat myself by the ocean on the beach I found some packages of peanuts right before me.

The beautiful Ada began to snap them.

She hummed a jaunty ditty. Her head inclined pathetically against my shoulder. My hair, stirred by the sea zephyrs, patted her cheek.

She said the song was "My Gal's a High-Born Lady."

Who was its author? Emerson did not write it surely.

When I returned to the hotel, I undertook to place on the wall the weather-torn fragment of cotton which I had picked up at the park.

These words were printed on it:

> "KEEP OFF
> THE GRASS"

I decided to mail it to my Japan, requesting my daddy to post it upon my garden grasses—somewhere by the old cherry tree.

9th—To-day is the third anniversary of my grandmother's death.

I will keep myself in devotion.

I burned the incense I had bought from a Chinaman. I watched the beautiful gesticulation of its smoke.

Good Grandma!

She wished she could live long enough to be present at my wedding ceremony. She prayed that she might select the marriage equipage for me.

I am alone yet.

I wonder if she knows—does her ghost peep from the grasses?—that I am drifting among the ijins she ever loathed.

I don't see how to manage myself sometimes—like an unskilful fictionist with his heroine.

When shall I get married?

10th—I yawned.

Nothing is more unbecoming to a woman than yawning.

I think it no offence to swear once in a while in one's closet.

I was alone.

I tore to pieces my "Things Seen in the Street," and fed the waste-paper basket with them.

The basket looked so hungry without any rubbish. An unkept basket is more pleasing, like a soiled autograph-book.

"I didn't come to Amerikey to be critical, that is, to act mean, did I?" I said.

I must remain an Oriental girl, like a cherry blossom smiling softly in the Spring moonlight.

But afterwards I felt sorry for my destruction.

I thrust my hand into the basket. I plucked them up. They were illegibly as follows:

> " women coursing like a
> 'rikisha of 'Hama   their children
> crying at home   left somewhere
> their womanliness
> gentleman with stove-pipe hat   blowing
> nose with his fingers   young
> lady   kept busy chewing gum
> while walking. If you once show such a grace
> at Tokio, you shall wait fruitlessly for the
> marriage offer.
> "   old grandma in gay red skirt
>   aged man arm-in-arm with wife
> so young   What a martyrdom
> to marry for G-O-L-D!   policeman
> has no
> "San Francisco is a beautiful city, but
> 'vertisements of 'The Girl From Paris'
>   W— —d's Beer
> with the watches hanging on their breasts
>   God bless you, red necktie
> gentleman   woman at the corner
> chattering like a street politician."

And I missed some other hundred lines.

11th—A letter from the minister arrived.

(I'd be a postman, by the way, if I were a man. A noble work that is to deliver around the love and "gokigen ukagai.")

I clipped off the Mexican stamp.

I will make a stamp book for my boy who may be born when I become a wife.

Before opening the letter I pressed it to my ear. My imaginative ear heard his illustrious "Ha, ha, ha——" rolling out.

How I missed his happy laughter!

Can he now pronounce a "How do?" in Mexican?

12th—It surprises me to learn that many an American is born and dies in a hotel.

Such a life—however large rooms you may possess—is not distinguishable, in my opinion, from that of a bird in a cage.

Is hotel-living a recent fashion?

Don't say so!

The business locality—like the place where this Palace Hotel takes its seat—does not afford a stomachful of respectable air.

I preferred some hospitable boarding house in a quiet street, where I might even step up and down in nude feet. I wished to occupy a chamber where the morning sun could steal in and shake my sleepy little head with golden fingers as my beloved mama might do.

We will move to the "high-toned" boarding house of Mrs. Willis this afternoon.

Her house is placed on the high hill of California Street.

I am grateful there is no car quaking along there.

My uncle says I shall have a whole lot of millionaires for neighbours.

California must be one dignified street.

The Chinese colony is close at hand from Mrs. Willis',—the exotic exposition brilliant with green and yellow colour. The incense surges. So cute is the sparrow-eyed Asiatic girl—such a "karako"—with a small cue on only one side of the head. Dear Oriental town!

Good luck, I pray, my Palace Hotel!

Sayonara, my graceful butlers!

I shall hear no more of their sweet "Yes, Madam!" They talk gently as a lottery-seller.

The more they bow and smile the more you will press the button of tips.

They are so funny.

So long, everybody!

13th—The savour of the air is rich without being heavy.

The Tokio atmosphere emits a lassitude.

It's natural that the Japs are prone to languor.

A good while ago I pushed down my window facing the Bay of San Francisco. I leaned on the sill, my face propped up by both my hands.

The grand scenery absorbed my whole soul.

"Ideal place, isn't it?" I emphasised.

The bay was dyed in profound blue.

The Oakland boat joggled on happily as from a fairy isle. My visionary eyes caught the heavenly flock of seagulls around it.

If I could fly in their company!

The low mountains over the bay looked inexpressively comfortable, like one sleeping under a warm blanket.

The moon-night view from here must be wonderful.

I felt a new stream of blood beginning to swell within my body.

I buzzed a silly song.

I crept into my uncle's room.

I stole one stalk of his cigarettes.

I bit it, aping Mr. Uncle, when my door banged.

14th—I bustled back to my room.

My breast throbbed.

A naked woman in an oil painting stood before me in the hall.

Is Mrs. Willis a lady worthy of respect?

It is nothing but an insulting stroke to an Oriental lady—yes sir, I'm a lady—to expose such an obscenity.

I brought down one of my crape haoris, raven-black in hue,

with blushing maple leaves dispersed on the sleeves, and cloaked the honourable picture.

My haori wasn't long enough.

The feet of the nude woman were all seen.

I have not the least objection to the undraped feet. They were faultless in shape.

I myself am free to bestow a glimpse of my beautiful feet.

I turned the key of my door.

I stripped off my shoes and my stockings also.

Dear red silken stockings!

I scrutinised my feet for a while. Then I asked myself:

"Which is lovelier, my feet or those in the painting?"

15th—I couldn't rest last night.

The long wail of a horn somewhere in the distance—at the gate of the ocean perhaps—haunted me. The night was foggy.

I had a wild dream.

The fogs were not withdrawn this morning.

I was discouraged, I had to go out in my best gown.

Wasn't it a shame that two buttons jumped out when I hurried to dress up?

"Are the buttons secure?" is my first worry and the last.

Why don't Meriken inventors take up the subject of buttonless clothes?

Woman cannot be easy while her dress is fastened by only buttons.

16th—I wish I could pay my bill with a bank check.

Have I money in the bank with my name?

I fancied it a great idea to sleep with a big bank book under the pillow.

I decided to save my money hereafter.

How often have I expressed my hatred of an economical woman!

I detested the clinking "charin charan" of small coins in my purse. Very hard I tried to get from them.

Extravagance is a folly. Folly is only a mild expression for crime.

I deducted ten dollars from the fifty that I had settled for my new street gown. I dropped a card notifying my ladies' tailor that I had altered my mind for the second price.

"Ten already for the bank!" I said.

I took it to the "Yokohama Shokin Ginko" of this city.

I was given a little book for the first time in my life.

I thought myself quite a wealthy woman preserving my money in the bank.

I pressed the book to my face. I held it close to my bosom as a tiny girl with a new doll.

And I smiled into a looking-glass.

17th—I went to the gallery of the photographer Taber, and posed in Nippon "pera pera."

The photographer spread before me many pictures of the actress in the part of "Geisha."

She was absurd.

I cannot comprehend where 'Mericans get the conception that Jap girls are eternally smiling puppets.

Are we crazy to smile without motive?

What an untidy presence!

She didn't even fasten the front of her kimono.

Charm doesn't walk together with disorder under the same Japanese parasol.

And I had the honour to be presented to an extraordinary mode in her hair.

It might be entitled "ghost style." It suggested an apparition in the "Botan Toro" played by kikugoro.

The photographer handed me a fan.

Alas! It was a Chinese fan in a crude mixture of colour.

He urged me to carry it.

I declined, saying:

"Nobody fans in cool November!"

18th—We had a laugh.

Ada, my sweet singer of "My Gal's a High-Born Lady," accompanied me to a matinée of one vaudeville.

This is the age of quick turn, sudden flashes.

The long show has ceased to be the fashion. Modern people are tired of the slowness of old times which was once supposed to be seriousness.

Could anything be prouder than the face of the acrobat retiring after a perilous performance?

Woman tumbler!

I wondered how Meriken ladies could enjoy looking at such a degeneration of woman.

I was glad, however, that I did not see any snake-charmer.

What a delightful voice that negro had! Who could imagine that such a silvery sound could come from such a midnight face? It was like clear water out of the ground.

I was struck by a fancy.

I sprang up.

I attempted to imitate the high-kick dance.

I fell down abruptly.

"Jap's short leg is no use in Amerikey—can't achieve one thing. I am frankly tired of mine," I grumbled.

19th—The Sunday chime was the voice of an angel. The city turned religious.

Mrs. Willis—I had no curiosity about her first name; it is meaningless for the "Mrs." of middle age—indulged in chat with me.

If I say she was "sociable"?—it sounds so graceful.

She announced herself a bigot of poetry. She was bending to make a full poetical demonstration.

Of course it was more pleasing than a mourning-gowned narrative of her lamented husband. (I suppose he is dead, as divorce is too commonplace.)

But it were treachery, if I were put under her long recital of the insignificant works of local poets.

Tasukatta wa!

A little girl came as a relief.

41

Dorothy! She is a boarder of Mrs. Willis', the golden-haired daughter of Mrs. Browning.

(Mrs. Browning was a disappointment, however. I fancied she might be a relative of the poet Browning. I asked about it. Her response was an unsympathetic "No!")

"O' hayo!" Dorothy said, spattering over me her familiarity.

It takes only an hour to be friends with the Meriken girl, while it is the work of a year with a Japanese musume.

"Great girl! Your Nippon language is perfect! Would you like to learn more?" I said.

"I'd like it," was her retort.

Then we slipped to my room.

I wonder how Mrs. Willis fared without an audience!

I was sorry, thinking that she might regard me as an uncivil Jap.

"Chon kina! Chon kina!"

Thus Dorothy repeated. It was a Japanese song, she said, which the geisha girls sung in "The Geisha."

Tat, tat, tat, stop, Dorothy!

Truly it was the opening sound—not the words—of a nonsensical song.

I presume that "The Geisha" is practising a plenteous injustice to Dai Nippon.

I recalled one Meriken consul who jolted out that same song once at a party.

He became no more a gentleman to me after that.

20th—I pasted my little card on my door.

I wrote on it "Japanese Lessons Given."

I gazed at it.

I was exceedingly happy.

21st—A gardener came to fix our lawn.

There is nothing lovelier than verdant grasses trimmed neatly. They are like the short skirt of the Meriken little girl.

We women could be angels, I thought, if our speech lapped justly. Women talk superfluously. I do often.

What language did that gardener use?

It must be the English of Carlyle, I said, for its meaning was intangible.

I discovered, by and by, that German English was his honourable choice.

My eyes could express more than my English uttered in Nippon voice. My gestures helped to make my meaning plain.

He became my friend.

He carried a red square of cotton to wipe his mouth, like the furoshiki in which a Japanese country "O' ba san" wraps her New Year's present.

And again as he was leaving I saw a red thing around his neck. Was it not the same furoshiki which served for his nose?

It wouldn't be a bad idea to play amateur gardener.

The season wasn't fitting for such a performance, however.

A large summer hat! That was the customary attire.

But my light-hearted straw one with its laughing bouquet was not adapted to November, however gorgeously the sun might shine.

And it's sheer stupidity to track after a tradition.

I wound a large flapping piece of black crape about my head. (How awfully becoming the garb of a Catholic nun would be! I do not know what is dear, if it is not the rosary. A writhing rope around the waist is celestial carelessness.)

I appeared on the lawn, but without a sprinkler and rake. It would have been too theatrical to carry them.

I gathered the small stones from amid the grasses into a wheelbarrow near by.

Just as my new enterprise was beginning to seem so delightful, the luncheon gong gonged.

My uncle goggled from the hall, and said:

"Where have you been? I was afraid you had eloped."

"I've no chance yet to meet a boy," I spoke in an undertone.

Afterward I was ashamed that I had been so awkwardly sincere.

22nd—There was one thing that I wanted to test.

43

My uncle went out. I understood that he would not be back for some hours.

I found myself in his room, pulling out his drawer.

"Isn't it elegant?" I exclaimed, picking up his dress-suit.

At last I had an opportunity to examine how I would look in a tapering coat.

Gentleman's suit is fascinating.

"Where is his silk hat?" I said.

I reached up my arms to the top shelf of a closet, standing on the chair.

The door swung open.

Tamageta! My liver was crushed by the alarm.

A chambermaid threw her suspicious smile at me.

Alas!

My adventure failed.

23rd—I mean no one else but O Ada San, when I say "my sweet girl."

She was tremendously nice, giving a tea-party in my honour.

The star actress doesn't appear on the stage from the first of the first act. I thought I would present myself a bit later at the party, when they were tattling about my delay.

I delight in employing such little dramatic arts.

I dressed all in silk. It's proper, of course, for a Japanese girl.

I chose cherry blossoms in preference to roses for my hat. Roses are acceptable, however, I said in my second thought, for they are given a thorn against affronters.

I went to Miss Ada's looking my best.

They—six young ladies in a bunch—stretched out their hands. I was coaxed by their hailing smile.

Ada kissed me.

I had no charming manner in receiving a kiss before the people no more than in giving one. I blushed miserably. I knew I was bungling.

O Morning Glory, you are one century late!

They besieged me.

44

None of them was so pretty as Ada. Beauty is rare, I perceive, like good tweezers or ideal men.

I distributed my Japanese cards.

All of my new friends held them upside down.

Is it a modern vogue to be ignorant?

Ada played skilfully her role of hostess, which was a middle-aged part. She didn't even spill the tea in serving. Her "Sugar? Two lumps?" sounded fit. She divided her entertaining eye-flashes among us.

Tea is the thing for afternoon, when woman is excused if she be silly.

We all undressed our too-tight coat of rhetoric in the sipping of tea.

We laughed, and laughed harder, not seeing what we were laughing at.

I couldn't catch all of their names.

Such a delicious name as "Lily" was absurdly given to a girl with red blotches on her face.

(A few blemishes are a fascination, however, like slang thrown in the right place.)

Her flippancy was like the "buku buku" of a stream.

Lightness didn't match with her heavy physique.

"How lovely an earthquake must be!" she chirruped. "Shall I go to Japan just on that account? A jolly moment I had last February. A baby earthquake visited here, as you know. I was drinking tea. The worst of it was that I let the cup tumble on to my pink dress. I prayed a whole week, nevertheless, to be called again."

Woman has nothing to do with a hideous make-up. Miss Lily should not select a pink hue.

"You are awful!" I said.

I told about the horror of a certain famous Japanese earthquake. They all breathed out "Good heavens!"

There was one second of silence.

Ada struck a gushing melody on the piano.

The lively Meriken ladies prompted themselves to frisk about.

I was ready to cry in my destitution.

One girl hauled me up violently by the hand.

"Come and dance!"

Her arm crawled around my waist, while she directed:

"Right foot—now, left!"

I returned to Mrs. Willis', my thoughts absorbed in a dancing academy.

"I must learn how to skip," I said.

24th—I hate the alarm clock, simply because it is always so punctual.

"I was too late" is a delightful expression.

"Mrs. Willis' breakfast is at quarter-past eight!"

Isn't that "quarter-past" interesting?

And I can never be ready before nine.

25th—I dragged my uncle off to the Chute to enrich my store of zoology.

"One gape more, Uncle, to count up one dozen!" I said, and pulled his mustache in the car.

It was lucky that no one saw my act.

Poor Oji San! Playing chaperon is not a very promising occupation, is it?

I stood by the "happy family" of monkeys. I tried to descry their point of view in orations.

I gave it up.

The vain Miss Polly worked hard to bring everybody to an understanding with one eternal "Hello, dear!"

I found such grace in the elephant when he waved his honourable trunk.

The stupid Mr. Elephant wasn't stupid a bit in accepting my present.

How philosophically he gazed at me! Very likely I was the first Jap girl to his audience.

What respectable eyes!

"You'll bankrupt yourself in peanuts," my uncle warned.

26th—A white apron on my black dress makes me so cute.

I am just suited to be a chambermaid. Shall I volunteer as a servant?

I bought an apron.

To-day is house-cleaning day.

I kept busy a good while arranging my theatrical costume as a maid.

Wasn't it fun?

I was ready to scrub the floor, when I heard "kotsu kotsu," on my door.

It was Annie with a broom.

"I'm your help. Just a moment! I have forgotten the finishing glance in my mirror."

27th—I have been studying the catechism.

I am afraid to go to church, for the minister may put many a question to me.

Is Miss Ada a dutiful church-goer?

I don't think so.

She would rather mumble a nigger song than a chapter from the Bible.

I will ask her a few things from the catechism at my first opportunity.

28th—"Hand me your cup after you are done with your tea!" Mrs. Browning requested. "I will ponder on your fortune."

"How delightful!" I said.

My fortune?

I remembered how I used to scatter my pocket money among the fortune-tellers, pleased to be informed of a lot of nice things.

What meaning she could find in a cup!

I felt like a mother with her children already in bed, when I dropped my spoon into my tea.

I felt mistress of the situation.

Was there ever anything more welcome than to learn your fortune?

"A young American (rich, very rich—indeed) will win your affection. The marriage will be a happy one," she prophesied.

Is that so?

Life is becoming very interesting.

I wonder where my would-be husband is seeking me.

Shall I advertise in a paper?

How?

If my first-rate picture by Mr. Taber were printed, it would be a whole thing in such a business.

I thought the picture beautiful enough to sell at any stationer's of U.S.A.

How many thousand could I sell in a week?

Could I make money out of it? Some decent fortune, I mean, of course.

29th—Ho, ho, such a day!

I was aroused by the roar of a milk-wagon early in the morning.

I sought a pin in vain.

I tore my skirt on a sneering nail at the door.

I upset my flower-vase.

I sat by my window. A vegetable pedlar howled to me, "Potatoes? Potatoes?"

I couldn't recall a sweet dream I had last night.

The clamour of a Chinese funeral passed under my room. The carriages were packed with hired "crying women." Isn't it a farce?

I went out. My street-car ran off the track.

A fire-engine deafened me.

I passed by an undertaker's. It was cold like a grave.

The sight stunned me.

30th—Is my nose high enough?

I bought a pair of "nose spectacles."

Those with wires to circle the ears, which are Oriental (that is to say old-fashioned), would suit even a noseless Formosa Chinee.

But how many Japs could show themselves ready for nose spectacles?

The Optician asked if they were for myself.

He was a trifle uncertain about my nose, I suppose.

"No! For my friend," I said.

It was a white lie.

I blushed as if I had committed a heavy crime.

I hoped I had not.

I put my new spectacles on my nose, as soon as I returned to my room. Very well they stayed. Mother Nature was specially kind to me.

But what a depression—also what torture—I felt from their clutch!

I was pleased, however, seeing myself somewhat scholarly.

Aren't spectacles an emblem of wisdom?

The first requirement to be a critic should be spectacles. The second is a pessimistic smile, of course.

My mirror told me that I looked quite modern.

"Book!" I exclaimed.

I must see what effect I could produce with a book on my lap.

I leaped from the chair to fetch one.

My spectacles dropped from my honourable nose on to the hearthstone. My nose was exceedingly stupid.

Alas, and alas!

The spectacles were crushed to pieces.

I was broken also.

I buried my face in the pillow for some time.

Then I said: "I'm not short in my sight. I have no use for them except for fun."

I wiped my disturbed eyes with a handkerchief. My finger felt the rude marks printed on both sides of my nose.

Dec. 1st—I bought a Louisiana lottery ticket through Annie.

Like any other domestic girl, she has no key to her mouth. She is like a sentence that has forgotten to add the period.

I begged all sorts of gods to drop the capital prize on me.

Thirty thousand dollars! Think!

How shall I manage with them when I have won?

2nd—If I were a painter!

My eyes were fixed upon the dying sun. Its solemnity was like the passing of a mighty king.

Some time glided by.

My thought was pursuing the sun.

The twilight!

Oh, twilight pacifying me as with the odour from a magical palace!

Hush!

The melody of a piano effused from my neighbour.

The best thing in the world is to play music. The very best is to listen to the profuse melody evoked by a master.

Was it a superb execution?

My soul was dissolved, anyhow, in the rapture.

I left my uncle's room where I saw the grand sun pass away.

I put me in my bed, because my visionary mood was not to be stirred for the world, and because I wished to dream a romance without the delay of a moment.

But I could not slumber.

And I missed my dinner.

I petitioned my uncle to step out into the street for my beloved chestnuts.

Dear Italian chestnut vendor!

I never pass by without buying.

3rd—We start to-morrow for Los Angeles of Southern California.

Mr. and Mrs. Schuyler have invited us to spend some weeks with them.

The gentleman was the former consul at Yokohama. My uncle is his intimate friend.

My new trunk was brought in from the store.

It bears my name in Roman of commanding type.

I stared at the characters as upon an ancient writing whose meaning could only be imagined.

"Doesn't 'Miss Morning Glory' suggest that the owner is a charming young lady?"

My little smile smiled, as I thought that it would, of course.

A new trunk, I am sorry to say, lacks a historical look. An old one is more gratifying, like old brocade or an old ring.

Au revoir, my Ada!

South-bound train, 4th—I was lavish of my art of "bothering."

My poor uncle—my eternally "poor uncle" was the victim. I wanted some diversion at any price.

His face scowled as I bored him with my successive questions.

I thought his irritated face fascinating.

When I presented another question, he was droning a genteel snore.

I twisted an edge of a newspaper into a roll. I thrust it into his nose.

There was no doubt about his starting.

"Bikkurishita!" he exclaimed.

Then he begged to be allowed some chance to rest.

This is a "bad year for cucumbers" for him. He made a mistake in accompanying me on Meriken Kenbutsu.

Honestly I have to behave nicely.

My opening question to Uncle was: "What's the derivation of 'damn'?"

"Imperialism" was my last.

I have a high regard for the people dignified by using the capital "I" for the personal pronoun.

But if I were the President I should not wish to be addressed with that hackneyed, unromantic "Mr."

The cartoonists making sport of the President shock me.

How big-hearted the President is!

Those "devils" would be beheaded in the Orient.

Los Angeles, 5th—No one bangs the door at Schuyler's.

The servants drop their eyes meekly before they speak.

A well-bred atmosphere circulates.

A woman over forty-five is nothing if she isn't motherly enough to let one feel at home. Mrs. Schuyler's silence is a smile. I loved her from my first glance. I thought I could ask her to wash my hair some sunny day. I could fancy how pleasant it would be to

51

immerse myself in her chat—such sort of talk as an old-bonneted "how to keep house"—while I was drying my hair in the indolence of a sea-nymph. Modern topic is like black coffee, it is too stimulating. There is nothing dearer than a domestic subject.

I have no hesitation in accepting her as my Meriken mother.

I am positive I would feel more comfortable if I had one in this country.

How good-naturedly she was fattened!

A somewhat stout woman looks so proper for a mother.

I wished I could lean on her plump shoulder from the back in Japanese girl's way, and play with her hair, and ask a few innocent questions like "What have I to eat for dinner?"

She talked about the Japanese woman, principally praising her shapely mouth.

I felt conceitedly, because I was given one classical little mouth, if I had nothing else to be noticed.

Mr. Schuyler grasped my hand ever so hard. My hand was buried in his palm. His manner was courteously boyish.

His body is erect like a redwood.

Such an old gentleman gives me the impression of another race from the divine realm of everlasting youth. A Jap after fifty is capped with "retired."

But the work of the American gentleman is only finished when he dies.

Great Meriken Jin!

Mr. Schuyler shows more civility to his servants than to his wife.

Here I can study the typical household of America's best caste.

6th—"Anata donata?"

I rubbed my dreamy eyes, scanning my room.

Who was the Japanese speaker?

I crept to the door, and opened it slightly.

Not a soul was there.

I heard the trivial clatter of the kitchen stepping up.

I dipped into my bed again. I smiled sceptically, thinking that I must have been dreaming.

"Gokigen ikaga?"

I was addressed again by the same voice.

I said that there was positively some mischief in my room.

I leaped down from the bed.

I inspected my slippers. I made sure there was nothing strange under the pictures on the wall. I tugged at the drawers. I tumbled every blanket. I pried in the pitcher.

I sat on the bed wrapped in fog.

The blind rustled.

The sunbeams crawled in marvellously.

Then I was frightened by another speech, "Nihonjin desu."

I declared that it flew in from the outside.

I rolled up the blind.

Oya, oya! There was a parrot perching in a cage by my window!

He adjusted his showy coat first, and then sent me his inquisitive eyes.

"Anata donata?" he repeated.

"Morning Glory is my insignificant name, sir," I replied.

A trifling toss of his head showed his satisfaction in my name. I thought he was trying to set me at ease with his smile.

"Gokigen ikaga?"

"I feel splendidly, thank you, Mr. Parrot!" I said.

Then pressing his head backward he looked haughtily at me with fixed eyes, and announced:

"Nihonjin desu."

"I'm also a Jap," I muttered.

He was the most profound Japanese scholar, Mrs. Schuyler said, in all Los Angeles. Mr. Schuyler Jr. brought him from Kobe last spring.

I told her the incident of this morning.

She laughed, she said she expected it.

Bad Mother Schuyler!

17th—Dear Baby! Kawaii koto!

I hugged the baby of Mrs. Schuyler Jr. and kissed it.

Her husband is away in Japan for the tea business.

53

It was the darling baby, I thank the gods, who received my first kiss.

It's heavenly to stamp love with a kiss. Lips are the portal of the human heart.

Kiss is sweet.

I say that it marks an epoch in the spiritual evolution of the Japanese when they learn what a kiss is—but not how to kiss.

The baby crawled like a sportive crab. It orationed. It! I felt sorry that "It" would soon be changed to "He" or "She." It caught sight of a piece of burnt match in the course of its expedition. It turned its way and clinched it with its fingers. It hastened to the mother to exhibit it, and waited patiently with its great game for Mamma's praise.

I nearly cried in my excitement at such a pathetic revelation.

Lovely thing!

The baby had blue eyes.

My preference wasn't for blue eyes. I often snapped at them, saying that they were like a dead fish's eyes.

But how long can I keep up my ill-will, when I look with delight upon the blueness in water, sky and mountain?

Isn't it precious to see the blue pictures on china?

A blue pencil is just the thing to mark on the margin of a pleasing book.

Blue is a poetical hue.

Robert Burns was blue-eyed.

I recalled the first American I met in Tokio, who seriously questioned whether it was a fact that Japs butcher a blue-eyed baby.

Bakabakashii wa!

Japan has no blue eye.

And Japanese are worshippers of any sort of baby.

If American babies were like Chinese girls!

I would pile up all my coins to buy one.

Meriken baby understood how to smile before how to cry. It is a lady or gentleman already.

I will serve as baby's nurse if I must support myself.

It's a high task to be useful to the baby, and watch its growth as a silent astronomer watches the stars.

I wish I could roll the baby's carriage day after day.

How sweetly the world would be turning then!

Shall I hire Schuyler's baby for one day?

8th—Is there any more gratifying word than dinner?

I had a "hipp goo'" dinner. (Permit a Chinese-English expression for once.)

Its inviting heaviness was like an honourable poem by Milton.

Schuyler's house has a Miltonic presence.

Electric light is too imposing.

Candelabra are like a moon whose beams are a lenitive song.

The nude shoulders of Mrs. Schuyler, Jr., crimsoned in the rays from the candelabra.

The exposure of some part of the skin is the highest order of art. How to show it is just as serious a study as how to clothe it.

If I had such supreme shoulders as hers, I would not pause before displaying them.

What falling shoulders are mine!

The slope of the shoulders is prized in Japan. Amerikey is another country, you know.

I appeared at the dinner in my native gown.

The things on the table had a high-toned excellence.

I will not forget to have my initials engraved if I happen to buy any silver.

Coffee was served. I felt that an old age had returned, when eating was only a dissipation.

I'm growing to love Meriken food.

I am glad that I don't see any musty pudding at Schuylers', a sight that makes me ten years older.

And another thing I hate is the smell of cabbage.

How pleased I was to see a "chabu chabu" of shallow water in my finger bowl! Just a glimpse of water is tasty.

Our taciturn butler retired from the dining-room with graceful dignity.

The butler has ceased to be a common servant. He has advanced, I suppose, to the rank of an ornament of the Meriken household.

The sister of Mother Schuyler and her husband dined with us.

The funniest thing about her was that she kept a few long hairs on her cheek. They grew from a mole.

It may be good luck to preserve them.

Her husband was surprised when he heard that we do not use knife and fork at home.

Bamboo chop-sticks! How dear!

9th—I have no belief in the earring.

It is a savage mode, like the deformed feet of the Chinese woman.

But why did the Meriken lady discard her veil?

Her face behind the veil would appear like a rose through the Spring mist. It is a charming thing as ever was fashioned for woman.

I have seen no lady with a veil in this town.

I suppose the Los Angeles women confide in their faces.

They strew more liberty in their grace than the San Franciscans.

Their beauty is informal.

The city is enchanting.

I am pleased that I am not shown here so many a "To Let" as in Frisco.

Even the barefooted Arabs, those street sparrows, are quite a picture.

10th—I promised Mrs. Schuyler, Jr., good care of her baby for half an hour.

I carried it firm on my arms.

I jogged out to the garden.

The baby faced toward me and said:

"Bu, bu! Bu, bu, bu!"

I felt grateful, thinking that it counted me among its friends.

I laid its head on my breast.

I sang a little Japanese lullaby:

"Nenneko, nenneko,
Nennekoyo!
Oraga akanbowa

Itsudekita?
Sangatsu sakurano
Sakutokini!
Doride okawoga.
Sakurairo."

(Sleep, sleep, sleep! When was our baby made? Third month, when the cherry blossoms. So the honourable face of our child is cherry-blossom coloured.)

The breezes billed and cooed upon the grasses. An imperial palm cast its rich shadow.

The affectionate sunlight made me think of a "little Spring" of the Japanese September. Everything inclined to a siesta in the yellow air.

A tropical touch is the touch of passion.

Can you fancy this is the month of December?

I cannot.

After I put the baby to its nurse, I paced around a bronze statue upon the lawn, losing myself in Greek beauty.

Then I snatched a rose.

I pressed it to my nose-tip.

12th—Where's my painstaking description of Echo Mountain?

I made a pleasant trip there yesterday with Schuyler's party.

I lost my writing penned last night.

Such a heedless tomboy!

I idled, watching a spider from my window. It was framing a net amid the garden trees. An awfully dignified tom cat glared from under a bush. I was sorry no game came upon the scene to his honour. My profound Japanese scholar was not discouraged by the lack of an audience. He was busy presenting his polite "Gokigen ikaga?"

Then I found what I did with my yesterday's diary.

Areda mono!

I wiped my oily hands with it and buried it in a trash basket.

I fixed my hair this morning.

Morning Glory San, you have to keep your Nikki in a safe!

57

Great Carlyle wrote his "French Revolution" twice.
I wish I had been given a slice of his persistency.

13th—A Bishop visited and lunched with us.
Bishop! How I desired to meet one!
It had been my fancy, ever since I read of the venerable Bishop who threw out candle-sticks to Jean Valjean in Hugo's book.
His name was Myriel.
What is my friend's name? After a man reaches the bishop's see, his own name should retire from actual service. People call him "Bishop! Bishop!" as if it were a nickname.
My bishop had a holy face.
"Who is this good man who is staring at me?" I said to myself at first sight, as Napoleon said when he saw Myriel.
A young churchman is unnatural.
The customarily pessimistic face of the Japanese priest causes aversion.
I got what I wanted in my new friend.
If I were his daughter, I would comb his silken hair before he goes to church on Sunday.
I was glad he was not thin.
Ho, ho, ho! He ate meat like anybody else.
He would seem holier if he merely bit a crust of bread, and sipped three spoonfuls of tea.
After luncheon we strolled through the garden arm in arm.
Not a bit I blushed. I was as completely at ease with him as with my papa.
He told me of the beauty of Christ. His soft, deep voice was as from a far-away forest.
I plucked a few stems of violets. I fitted them to his buttonhole.
Such a little thing pleased him immensely.
Dear, simple Bishop!
I digested what he spoke. I declared that Christianity was the sun, while Buddhism was the moon.
The sun is day and life, and the moon night and rest.
How can we live without the sun? The moon is poetry.

58

14th—The sky became low, its colour frowning gray.

The winds snarled.

December was suddenly calling us.

We sat by a snug fire at evening.

Its yellow flame suggested a preacher uplifting his hands in prayer. The fire flickered in jollity.

"Pachi, pachi, pachi!"

The parlour was not lighted.

The pictures on the wall were impressive in the firelight.

Any woman looks charming at night and by the fireside. I felt happy imagining that I must appear lovely.

The fireplace is so dear, like mamma's lap.

Mr. Schuyler brought a chess-board and challenged.

I offered me for a fight.

I used to play American chess with a Meriken missionary who lived in my neighbourhood. I thought it fun to beat an old man.

"Namu Tenshoko Daijingu!" I repeated.

The gentleman asked what I muttered.

"Never mind! Only a little spell!" I replied in the lightest fashion.

The chess-board was placed between us.

"Mr. Schuyler, can you sacrifice anything for the game?"

"Whatever you please, my little woman!"

"Well!"

"Well, then!"

"Suppose you make Mrs. Schuyler your stake! My uncle will be mine."

"Ha, ha! Very well!"

He was a tactician. I fought hard.

Alas, my game was lost!

My second stake was myself.

"It means that I may marry you, doesn't it?"

"As you please, sir!"

Iyani natta!

He was far superior.

Oya, oya, I was a loser again!

I looked sadly on my uncle, and said:

"Uncle, you cannot return home! We are the property of Mr. Schuyler. Isn't it really too bad?"

15th—Shall I make a little kimono for Schuyler's baby?

It would be a souvenir of my visit.

The crape kept in the Jap stores of this town isn't appropriate for a baby's "bebe." My flower-dyed under-kimono should be utilized.

I opened my trunk.

Mother Schuyler brought in a young lady. She was her niece, that is to say the daughter of Mrs. Ellis. Mrs. Ellis is the one with the long hair on her cheek.

I told them of my new drift.

They were surprised at my determination.

Miss Olive applied to be my pupil in Japanese sewing.

What a southern name! Olive perfectly fits for a girl born in the passionate breeze.

Her "Is that so?" or "Don't you?" fluttered affectionately like golden sunshine.

Mrs. Schuyler bade her servant to move in the machine.

I objected.

Machine-clicking is not Oriental. The "bebe" has to be done in pure Japanese.

16th—I found a hammock on the veranda.

It is the thing for summer, of course.

I never laid me in it before in my life.

I thought that I would see how I would feel.

I hanged it.

I romped in it.

It was delightful. I fancied that we—I and who?—hammocked among the summer breezes. Then a star appeared. He said, "How beautiful the star is!"

What did I fancy next?

Oh, never mind!

I tossed my feet. The skirt fluttered. My new satin slippers—

number one and a half—were all seen. I drew up my skirt a little, and made a whole show of my honourable legs.

I prayed that somebody would pass by to fling an adoring glance at them.

No one roamed along. I scorned my frivolity.

The Bible by me wasn't open at all.

I decided to read it to-day, although religion isn't so becoming.

My Bishop sent it this morning. Dear old Bishop! He thought me quite a docile "nenne."

I stretched my body in the hammock.

Alas, ma!

My hana kanzashi with the butterflies was caught by the meshes. The wings of one butterfly were tortured. Yes, I had put a Japanese pin on my hair this morning.

I hoped I could pay a bit more attention to my head all the time.

I was sad for a while.

17th—Good Annie wrote me from Mrs. Willis'.

What a scrawl!

But woman's bad grammar and infirm penmanship are pathetic, don't you think so?

It might look better on a thin blue tablet.

But poor Annie chose such thick smooth paper.

Oya! What?

A five-dollar check?

My goodness, I had forgotten all about my lottery! Even the ticket I have lost. It drew out five dollars.

Why not thirty thousand dollars?

It was better than a blank, anyway, I said philosophically.

Now let me send a little present to my home!

A little thing is a deal sweeter.

I ordered fourteen packets of N. Y. Central Park lawn seed from a nursery.

New York Central Park!

Doesn't it sound grand?

And other flower seeds also.

61

The dwarf sweet pea is named "Cupid."

It will be no wonder if my father mistakes it for a kibisho.

Cupid is a handsome boy, not a bullfrog-looking teapot, funny papa!

He is garden crazy. I can imagine how conceited he will be showing around his western sea flowers when they are in bloom.

I asked my uncle to translate the directions.

Isn't it handy to keep a secretary?

I'll not miss signing my name on the translation.

My daddy may think it was done by myself.

Woman is a snob.

Now what for mamma?

18th—Mother Schuyler took me to her church.

Such a heathen me!

I felt that I was "sitting on needles," when I slipped into the Meriken church without glancing at even one page of the Bible. It was as risky a venture as to face an examination before fitting.

The service hadn't begun.

Many ladies were introduced to me by Mrs. Schuyler.

They talked about—what?—anything but religion.

I was fanned continually by an offensive odor. Some one had left her perfume at home.

Honourable arm-pit smell!

Amerikey cultivates many a disagreeable sort of thing, doubtless.

The ladies seemed to regard the church as another drawing parlor.

My mind was calmed within ten minutes.

Ureshiya!

The Meriken church is not a difficult place at all.

A Japanese church is ever so sad-faced. No woman under thirty is seen there. I laughed at the thought of an "incense-smelling" young girl.

Isn't it strange that Meriken girls love the church?

Is it because they cannot marry without it?

Sunday amusement doesn't begin before noon. What would girls do if there were no church where they could burst into song?

How classically the bald head of the minister shone!

There is nothing more pleasing than a sweeping sermon on a bright day.

But my mind strayed, wondering why all those ladies were so homely.

I snatched my hat off, wishing to be different from the rest.

I fancied the reason why their hats were eternally glued to their heads was because their hair was never in first-rate order for exhibition.

Many years ago I used to steal into a Buddha temple, being a little "otenba," and tap an idol's shoulder, saying: "How are you getting along, Hotoke Sama?"

Not one idol here!

No incense!

How uninteresting!

How silly I was inventing some clever thing for the occasion when I should be forced to confess! The church was not Catholic.

When we returned home, Mrs. Schuyler asked me what was the text.

"Let me see——"

I made as if I had been a listener to the sermon.

"Dear Mrs. Schuyler, what was it?" I exclaimed as if I had accidentally forgotten.

19th—Miss Olive offered to show me how to play golf.

I went to her home at Pasadena.

Pasadena is a luxurious Winter resort of cheerful aspect.

Its water is blessed.

Even the street cars run like a well-bred gentleman. The dog never growls around. It only wags its tail. No beggars.

America's outdoor diversion demands a great deal of strength.

What an imbecile "anego!"

After fifteen minutes I found two bean-like blisters on each palm.

I gave up the game.

I bought a golf outfit, nevertheless, in a store on my way home. The sight of a lady carrying it once stamped itself on my mind as so charming.

What attire would be becoming to me?

I said that my waist should be of deep red wool. Skirt? It must also be of wool, of course, with a large checkerboard pattern. Silk isn't gamesome, is it? And the hat should be a mouse-coloured felt, which must be thrust carelessly by my big gold pin with a coral head.

I well-nigh decided to dye my hair red.

What will my uncle say?

20th—Schuyler's cook wasn't acquainted with the art of rice-cooking.

Mother Schuyler said explanatorily that she had never tasted properly cooked rice since the day at Yokohama.

The rice was pasty.

I thought I would boil the rice according to Japanese prescription for to-day's dinner.

I stepped down to the kitchen.

I put three cupfuls of rice in a saucepan, and dipped my hand in it, and supplied water as much as to my wrist.

I placed it on the splendid fire till the agitated water pushed up the lid. Then I moved it on to a gentle fire. The cooking was done after twenty minutes.

I was honoured by everybody at the dinner. The rice was singularly fine. The grains kept their own perfect shapes.

After the dinner I approached Mrs. Schuyler with ink and paper.

"Will you write your recommendation of my rice-cooking?" I said.

She gazed at me questioningly.

"What a funny girl! What shall I say?"

Then I dictated solemnly thus:

"To whom it may concern:

"I highly recommend Miss Morning Glory with her honourable art of rice-cooking. Her method is Japanese, that is to say, the best in the world.

Mrs. Schuyler"

21st:—Without a nephew Mother Schuyler wouldn't be a complete old dear.

She has one fortunately.

Olive San told me a whole lot about her great brother.

He is a promising artist.

Artist?

Doesn't an artist affect boorish hair? I was anxious to know how his hair was, because I hated anything long except a frock-coat.

Miss Olive declared him one handsome boy. (I thought how ridiculous is the American girl to praise her brother. It is Japanese etiquette to undervalue one's relatives in describing them.)

I finished my imaginary sketch of his face before we intruded in his studio.

Olive presented me to him.

He was a comely young man.

What gratified me most about him was his shapely shoes, well-polished.

He knew how to talk with girls.

I was instantly put on unceremonious terms.

How beautifully he once slipped "Miss" in addressing me! His gracefully-sounding "Pardon me, I mean Miss Morning Glory!" pleased me enormously.

I told him that it was a regular humbug to be particular.

"I will call you Oscar, shall I?" I said, winking.

I felt some fervid water oozing down my cheeks. I was blushing.

I was glad that he was not Mr. Ellis, Jr. The word "Jr." appears to me like a ragged papa's old coat which is dreadfully out of fashion.

"Will you let me paint you?" he requested.

"Am I beautiful enough, do you think?" I said, dropping my eyelids.

"Only too charming!" he said bravely.

I always think every gentleman whom I meet falls in love with me.

I regarded Mr. Oscar Ellis already as an adorer.

O sentimental Morning Glory!

When I returned to Schuyler's my mind was completely occupied with an absurd fancy.

I was thinking what I shall do when he proposes to me. Shall I say yes?

For a girl to fall in love with one while she is staying at his aunt's isn't romantic a bit, is it?

I don't care, anyhow, for an artist lover.

It is a worn-out hero in old fiction.

Doesn't the word "artist" ring like a synonym for poverty?

22nd—Mrs. Ellis invited me to dinner.

I went to Pasadena with Mrs. Schuyler, Jr.

The evening was fragrant.

After the dinner we stepped out to the garden. It was dusky.

By and by, twenty Japanese lanterns were candled among the trees in my honor.

I was in a sprightly bent.

I was whispering a little Jap song, when Oscar led out two donkeys.

Olive sprang upon the back of one in gracious audacity.

"Jump, Morning Glory!" she exclaimed.

I was wavering about my action, when I felt Oscar's firm arms around my waist. My small body was lifted on to the donkey's by his careless gallantry.

What a sensation ran through me! It was the first occasion to put me into so close contact with a Meriken young man.

My skirt was caught by the saddle. I made a whole exhibition of my leg.

But I was glad the stocking was beautiful.

Oscar held my bridle, pacing by my side.

Alas!

My donkey acted awfully.

Did he take it as a degradation to be whipped by a Jap?

Suddenly it dropped its honourable rump. I should have been pitifully thrown out, if my arm had not seized Oscar's neck. I looked apologetically at him. He turned his delighted face.

I could not stay a minute longer.

When I got me off from the donkey, I observed the new moon over my right shoulder.

"Good luck!" Olive San said.

Why?

Mr. Oscar began to whistle somewhat as follows:

"Ho pop pop pop, ho pop pop pa!"

23rd—To-day is Mrs. Schuyler's reception day.

She set two Japanese screens in the drawing room, moving them from her chamber. She sprinkled a great lot of exotic bric-a-bric about.

She opened a regular Chinese bazar which expressed every poor taste. Such confusion!

I fancied she wanted the callers to recollect that she was Mrs. Ex-Consul of the Orient.

Japan teaches nothing but simplicity. Simplicity is the philosophy of art.

I wondered how she lived there without learning it.

Every inch of Schuyler's parlour means a heap of money.

But is there anything more displeasing than tasteless luxury? Sufficiency is grateful, but superfluity is nothing but offence.

I thought that Americans buy things because they love to buy, not because they have to buy.

Meriken jin has to study the high art of concealing.

The brown people look upon the scattering of things (however costly they be) as lower than barbarity. Japs believe in the sublimity of space.

Isn't it delightful to sit on the new matting of a Japanese guest-room? Its fresh whiteness used to cure my headache.

Isn't it taste to place just one seasonable picture on the tokonoma?

So many a Mrs. Brown and Mrs. Smith called.

They surrounded me.

I asked myself whether they paid a visit to Mother Schuyler or to me.

They incessantly threw the following questions at me:

"How do you like America?"

"How long do you expect to stay?"

Such an inquisitive Meriken woman!

I wished I had been bright enough to print a slip with my reply.

Each lady wore four rings at least.

Are they real things?

Diamond is hardly my choice. Haughtily cold, isn't it?

I declared that their shapeless fingers were not fit to show without embellishment.

If I had money for a ring I would use it for 365 pairs of silk stockings. Isn't it a joy to change every day?

Schuyler's baby made a hit with its kimono.

All the ladies kissed and kissed.

The baby wondered at their act, rolling its eyes.

Mother Schuyler was quite fussy with a little speech about the history of its Japanese gown.

Funny old dear!

24th—Mr. Oscar Ellis came to paint me.

Dear Oscar!

I have never before left my face alone for such a close scrutiny.

I was restless at first, fancying that he was gathering all my flaws.

Then it happened in my thought that his absorption had something of religious devotion in it.

I grew easy.

I began to feel like a star with all the admirers in the earth.

A garden tree sent its shadow through the window. The time passed as gracefully as a fairy on tiptoe. The air was purple.

Oscar San chatted freely.

I never took the part of a listener before in my life. I found listening honourable.

"So you like the Oriental woman?" I said.

He said American beauty was rather external, like a street shop window. He would like to know, he said, if there was any word more pathetic than "sayonara."

"Isn't the Japanese woman like it?" he asked.

I thought he was correct.

He continued:

"I read in a modern poet the following lines:

' .... full of whispers and of shadows,
Thou art what all the winds have uttered not,
What the still night suggesteth to the heart.'

Such is the vague Japanese beauty in my idea."

"I am not so nobly sweet, am I?" I exclaimed.

He cast a strong look, as if he were trying to put his final judgment upon me.

He moved his brush slowly on the canvas.

I bowed a profound bow.

"Gomen kudasai!" I said.

And I laid me on the floor, stretching out my legs.

25th—I bought two dolls.

One for Schuyler's baby, as my Christmas gift.

I slept with the other last night. I squeezed my ear to the dolly, fancying I might hear a few scratches of human voice. I kissed it. I laughed, saying that the doll was the thing for my starting to learn how to kiss.

"Sleep till mamma comes back, darling!" I said in the morning when I stepped down for my breakfast.

I left the table before I had half-finished, on account of my anxiety lest the upstairs girl might tattle of my childishness, if she found the doll in my bed.

Thank Heavens!

The girl hadn't come around yet.

I locked it up in my trunk.

What name shall I give it?

Charley?

I was disgusted at the thought, because every Chinee—ten thousand Mongols in all—is named one Charley.

Merry Christmas, all of you!

26th—It rained.

I implored Mother Schuyler to select a book from her library.

All the literature was packed in there, beginning with Socrates, sane as a silver dollar.

Every book was without finger-marks. Book without finger-mark is like bread without brown crust. Dear finger-mark!

The fashion is to buy books and to glance at their covers, I suppose, but not to read them. Modern publications aren't meant to be read, are they? The authors have degenerated to the place of upholsterers. Isn't it a shame?

Mrs. Schuyler picked out for me "Rubaiyat of Omar Khayyam."

My uncle said: "American woman can't keep away from Omar and chicken-salad."

I began to peruse it.

The raindrops by my window tuned:

"Tap, tap, tip, tap, tap!"

I thumped the book on the floor, and exclaimed:

"Mr. Khayyam!"

Rubaiyat is a menace against civilisation.

Americanism is nothing but the delight in life and the world.

I wonder why the wise government of Washington does not oppose its pagan circulation.

It is leprosy.

But I thought how truly true was his "I came like Water, and like Wind I go."

I took up the book and opened it again.

Then I shut it.

I listened to the "Tap, tap, tip!"

Doesn't it sound like a wan voice of Omar?

Yes!

27th—A lady whom I met at Mrs. Schuyler's reception sent me a mass of distinguished roses.

Loving American!

I said I would arrange them in Japanese cult.

My style is the enshin.

Amerikey is destitute of flowers.

Nippon is known as a paradise of botanists. The "scientists" of flower decoration (if I may call them so) are given a great advantage in their craft of delineating beauty.

The rose is not much of a flower to the Jap mind.

They never employ it in their work. It has no grace of line. Its perfume cannot indemnify for its being thorny. Things not qualified to convey charm are declined from the tokonama.

I love roses awfully well myself.

I will make the best of them in my art.

Is there any proper vase in Schuyler's house?

Mother Schuyler fetched me two pieces.

One was a silver vase and the other a china one.

I couldn't use them, I was sorry. Silver was commercial-looking. The painting on the china a hodge-podge of a joss house.

Then I was seized with a thought.

I ran down to the kitchen.

I borrowed an old scrubbing bucket.

"Such a soft antique hue!" I exclaimed with delight.

I elected one imperial rose and one little one for a "retainer."

I fixed them in the bucket.

I thought it was verily the simplicity of the illustrious Mr. Rikiu.

I presented the rest of the roses to Mrs. Schuyler, Jr.

She stared at the bucket without a word. I knew that her silence was the most forcible irony. She didn't approve of setting such a bucket on the table.

"Meriken jins don't know any art!" I said, when she left.

My uncle begged me not to act so fantastically.

28th—"Here's a shamisen, Morning Glory!" Mother Schuyler cried from the hall.

I darted out of my room.

"Well!" I exclaimed.

Shamisen?

It is a three-stringed guitar of Japan.

Mr. Schuyler, Jr., had sent it from Yokohama, as she explained.

She wished me to tinkle a little gamboling music in the parlour before dinner.

It is a hard implement to handle. It has no notation. Attainment is through unending blind practice.

I was compelled to learn by mother, many a year ago, but I soon gave it up for an English spelling-book.

But I daresay I can play.

I regulated the key to begin with.

"Ting, ting! Chang, Chang, ting!"

"What to hum, Uncle?" I asked, facing aside.

"Love ditty is desirable," Oji San considered.

"Don't fancy me a geisha!" I said in defending laughter.

Then I murmured an old hauta, "Haori kakushite," which was Englished by some one.

> "She hid his coat,
> She plucked his sleeve,
> 'To-day you cannot go!
> To-day, at least, you will not leave,
> The heart that loves you so!'
> The mado she undid
> And back the shoji slid:
> And clinging cried, 'Dear Lord, perceive
> The whole world is snow!'"

29th—We went to a theatre last evening.

Dear, classical "flower path"!

How I missed it in the Meriken stage!

Flower path?

It is a projection into the auditorium used to represent when one starts out of the house or returns.

So the American stage has no front gate scene! Every one enters very likely from the kitchen door.

The stage never turns round like the Japanese stage.

Oh, dear, iyadawa!

American play has too much kissing. Each time I was electrified.

The pit was filled with a well-behaved throng. All the ladies took off their hats. Do they pay more respect than in church? The gentlemen never whiffed smoke.

Japan theatre is a hurly-burly.

The "boys" roar up "Honourable tea—O'cha wa yoroshi? Honourable cake?" The attendants of tea houses bow around to the beneficent habitues, like inclining puppets.

Women sob. They laugh, stuffing their sleeves into their mouths. They are ready to put themselves in the play. They are sentimental.

Meriken women place themselves above the play.

I doubted whether they were criticising or enjoying.

Some lady even used a spy-glass to examine the face of a player.

I thought it decidedly an impertinence.

What a pry!

I will not act to such an assembly, if I ever happen to be an actress.

What was the title of the play?

I could hardly understand half of it.

I tried hard to swallow my gape.

30th—Mr. Oscar Ellis came to put the finishing touch to my picture.

The execution was subtle sureness.

He said that he would offer it to his beloved aunty—Mother Schuyler, of course—begging to let it ornament the wall of my room.

My room?

73

It is "my room" for a few days yet.

I thought it exceedingly sweet.

The wall is duskily red. The effect would be superb.

When I announced to him that our leave would take place on the approaching fourth, he started as if he had received a stroke.

"So soon?" he said.

"Yes," I said, turning my uneasy face.

"We are only beginning to understand each other."

"I am a bird of passage, as you know. I have to fly on my road."

The air grew tragic.

Then Oscar said:

"What will you do when you tire of flying?"

"Sah!"

"Well?"

"I'll return to Los Angeles and induce you to marry me with my honourable Oriental oratory. Will that do?"

We interchanged our nimble look. We laughed afterward.

After he left Schuyler's, I said to myself that I would not mind positively if he would kiss me. The kiss must be on my brow, however. Lips are too personal.

I wrote a note, beseeching him not to forget to kiss me at my farewell.

Then I chewed the note.

I reviled my folly.

31st—Street walking is a delight.

I'll mirror my face in the glass of the shop windows ambling by.

I dropped a handkerchief to-day.

A gentle gentleman—man behind me should be young and good looking always—picked it up. His respectful "Pardon me—" made me feel as if I were living in the silver-armoured age of chivalry.

Shall I drop something again?

I observed a variety of form in raising the skirt.

One lifted a bit of the left by her finger-tips. Another pulled up

74

the right edge of her front. Another clinched out the centre of her back, showing a significant fist. A corpulent one stepped, holding up both sides of her front. The miserable underskirt revealed itself in red.

Which mode is becoming to me?

Jan. 1st, 1900—Is to-day the opening of another century?

Happy New Year!

I will send a lot of "Shinnen omedeto" to Tokio.

Isn't this a queer New Year?

No shimenawa along the façades with flitting gohei!

No "gate pine tree"!

No sambow for an oblation unto the gods in any room!

No rice-bread! No golden toso for the cup!

I mingled with a neighbour's girls for a "rope-jumping."

We played hide-and-seek. I offered ten cents reward to the one who detected me. I abandoned the unprofitable job after emptying out all my change.

Miss Olive called on a bicycle.

I persuaded her to let me try on her bloomers. She exchanged them for my walking skirt which was four inches shorter.

We hurried to the garden.

She helped me on the wheel.

Such a bad Meriken girl!

She slipped her hand from it. I fell on a bush. The touchy rose thorned in my hand.

2nd—I made a discovery.

Mother Schuyler's teeth are all false.

I have no chance to explore whether her hair is a wig.

She chains a big bunch of keys to her waist. Its rattle sounds housewifely.

She forgot it, laying it on the sitting-room table.

I knotted it to my waist-strap.

I jiggled it.

"Jaran, jaring, jaran, jaran!"

3rd—The sayonara dinner was given. Mrs. Ellis' folks joined us.

Mother Schuyler repeated every ten minutes her query, "when would I visit them again?"

Mr. Oscar set his depressive look on me. I wasn't brave enough to encounter it.

I slid away from confronting him.

I found him an elegant young man. He impressed me as an image of Apollo.

Only God knows when I will reprint my footsteps on the soil of Los Angeles!

I felt awfully sorry in leaving such an agreeable company.

> "Fold your tent like the Arabs,
> And silently steal away."

How sad!

4th—Good-bye, Mr. Parrot!

San Francisco, 5th.

I am again at Mrs. Willis'.

San Francisco!

Such miraculous San Francisco water!

I will taste bliss again in drinking the midnight water, stretching out my arm from the bed.

6th—I tied Dorothy's hair in Nippon style.

She pleased me much by remembering the Japanese words I taught her.

She is a cute dear.

The mode had been the "O'tabaco bon."

I straightened her hair with my wet hand.

I added a tiny bit of crimson crape.

She looked a lovely fairy.

7th—Rainy day!

The heavily reserved weather confines me in the pose of genius.

My hair lounged down my shoulders. Disorder is the first step in being a genius, I fancy. My eyes should be rolled up to the sky in divine tragicalness.

I have had a greediness for the name of novelist.

To-day I found myself in the crisis where I must scribble or die.

I regret to say that mine is a love story also, as every beginner's book has been. I hope everybody will be contented with "The Destiny," a respectable title for my fiction. Who says it is the style of name employed one hundred years ago?

The book will be concluded with three hundred pages.

Now I wonder whether a long story is in demand.

Chapter I, is as follows:

WHEN THE MOON ROSE

This story begins when the moon rose.

Its silvery rays—it was six P.M. of April—fell on the Shiba park in laughter.

My heroine jogged along into the park, singing a light song.

> "Miss Honourable Moon, how old are you?
> Thirteen and seven, you say?
> You are young enough to marry— —"

Let me explain about her a bit!

Her name is O Hana San.

Thirteen years old. Thirteen? It is the age when the flower of girlhood starts to bloom.

Bewitching Hana!

Do you remember a well by the glorious cherry tree in the park? The 'rikisha men moisten their parched lips at the "Heaven-Sent." That is its name, sir.

Miss Hana looked down into the well.

She began to adjust her hair. The first worry of a girl after thirteen would naturally be about her hair.

She gazed up to the cherry blossoms and exclaimed:

"Utsukushii nah! Lovely!"

Then she found her face again in the well-mirror, thinking what a charming O Hana San it would make with the flowers on her hair.

My worthy readers, I suppose it is the time some one must enter.

He came.

He was a little boy.

I will not mention his name just yet.

He came close to her and pinched her little back. Both blushed, facing each other. They were quite strangers.

The evening zephyrs stirred the cherry blossoms. They planted themselves silently among the falling petals, as ethereal as snow.

"I delight to stand in the storm of petals, don't you?" Hana inclined her head a trifle in speaking.

The woman always speaks first.

"Let me see your school book!" again she said.

"Why?"

He put it in her tiny hand.

"Thanks! Arigato!"

She bowed low. When she put the book on her shoulder, she was running away, singing:

"Miss Honourable Moon, how old are you?"

The boy stood aghast.

****

The author of this story found O Hana San again by the same well on the next evening.

The boy's book in her hand, of course.

She paced around the well, muttering:

"He must come, because the moon rose."

But he was not seen.

My next chapter will be "The Second Meeting."

8th—My precious Ada again!

How could I live without her?

We hastened to a circus.

If I were a boy, I could earn a heap of money selling "Pea—nuts! Lemon—ade!"

How those clowns did tumble!

If I could share in such fun!

The ringmaster was the handsomest man in the world, in shiny boots and heavenly hat. How splendidly his whip cracked!

The clack dashed like a burst of bamboo.

"Wouldn't you be glad to be the lady on horseback? I would truly. Glance at her daring grace!" I whispered to Miss Ada.

Even the seal performed.

We laughed till tears dropped.

The circus had twenty elephants. Think!

Our Imperial Menagerie of Tokio has only one. How poor!

9th—Last night I went over to Mrs. Consul's to be given a lesson in card-playing.

"Cribbage would be the thing. Why? Because the Lambs took much pleasure in it," she said.

"How is poker?" I suggested.

"Gambling game!" she protested.

"I delight in gambling, Mrs. Consul," I proclaimed.

I had a wicked dream.

What do you imagine?

I ran away with a circus rider.

10th—I made the acquaintance of a Japanese woman.

She must have been passing her thirty springs. I could be accurate in my scale, being one of her sisterhood.

A cigar-stand keeper in Dupont Street.

Her name is O Fuji San.

Mrs. Wistaria brought a box of cigarettes that my uncle had ordered.

The morning is unoccupied in such a retail shop. Nobody puffs much before lunch. She set herself in a tête-à-tête.

The chastity of a wife may be measured by her solo on her husband. Woman's greatest joy often lies in lamenting the faults of her teishu.

Mrs. Wistaria spoke of her husband's being ill. I was to accept any chance for squandering my feelings. I sympathised, repeating, "Komaru nei! How sad!"

She said that she was going to leave the city for a week for the spring of San Jose, to take care of her infirm dear.

"I fear I may lose my customers," she flagged.

Her husband was afflicted with rheumatism.

I promised to call at her store.

Japs never visit an invalid without a present.

Champagne? It's too ostentatious a drink. It's like a highly rouged woman.

The loving-eyed claret should be chosen.

I sent half a dozen bottles to Mrs. Wistaria's.

A charity woman should be dressed in black and white. I went to Dupont street, however, in my grey dress.

Her husband struggled to entertain me. His clumsy smile appeared all the time at the wrong cue.

Poor Mr. What's-his-name!

Their business was an absurdly small affair.

The whole stock hardly valued above one hundred dollars.

I thought I could conduct it rightly.

I was carried away by a sudden fancy.

"Can't you leave your store in my hands, while you are away? Say yes! No?" I pressed myself upon them eagerly.

They were amazed.

"High-born lady like you? Oh, no! Doshite, doshite! Think! Do you know this is the toughest part of the town?" Mrs. Wistaria tried to make me retreat.

I couldn't listen to her, my whole soul being absorbed in my new caprice.

I thought it remarkably romantic.

I left the store to bring uncle to talk the matter over.

Mrs. Wistaria's store was neighboured by every saloon. The fuddling sounds overflowed in song:

"Hello ma baby, hello ma honey——"

11th—Now he is my beloved uncle.

He assured me of his help in carrying out my freak.

"You are fitting me for a slightly better rôle, I fancy," he said, venturing to add even one or two of his good-natured giggles. "The secretaryship of a cigar-stand is a rather more hopeful occupation than carrying your wraps through the street."

Everything was arranged.

Mrs. Wistaria and her husband set off for San Jose.

I am a merchant-lady.

The first thing I did was to put up a dignified sign with the following black letters:

MORNING GLORY CIGAR STORE

I borrowed a picture from Mrs. Willis' parlour, and placed it by the slot machine.

It is the picture of a dear Injun sitting against a woodland fire with a respectable pipe, whose smoke sails up to the yellow moon. What resignation! What dream! What joy! It did suit beautifully for the cigar-stand.

I love to see a man smoking. The elfish smoke acts like a merry-hearted May gossamer. When I observe a man's eye pursuing his smoke, I say to myself that his soul must be stepping nearer to his ideal. The road of smoke is the road of poesy.

A noble trade is tobacco.

Man's hermitage is situated only in smoking, I should say.

I divested my uncle of his coat. I begged him to hold a bucket and a piece of cloth for a moment.

"Are you ready to wash the windows, Uncle?" I said.

"Traitor, Morning Glory!" He flashed his accusing glare.

Docile old man!

He cleaned four windows of the kitchen, which was also the dining-room and the parlour.

I paid him five cents for each.

I said: "It's good fun to hire the chief secretary of the Nippon Mining Company to rub windows, isn't it?"

And I laughed.

Then I forced him to buy a cigar.

"You made some twenty cents out of me. Your turn is coming, my uncle!" I said.

I sold him a box of Lillian Russell cigars for three dollars. The real price was two.

Ha, ha, ha!

12th—I invited my precious Ada to my store to dine à la Japonaise.

One Jap restaurant catered to it.

"Irrashaimashi! Condescend to enter!" I showered my wooden-clogged greeting over Ada.

From "The Klondyke," my neighbouring saloon, a nigger song was flapping in.

"If you ain't got no money, you needn't come round."

Happy Ada San!

She was about to join in it, when I brought her into my great dining-room.

(Beg pardon, it was a paltry kitchen!)

Everything was seen on the table.

Japanese dinner has no strict order of courses. You are a frolicsome butterfly among the dishes set like flowers before you. You may flit straight to any one which catches your whim.

"Take your honourable chop-sticks!" I said.

Poor Miss Ada!

"How shall I manage with one stick?" she raised her eyelids in questioning meekness.

I bade her to split the stick in two. It was a brand new wooden one. I showed her how to finger it.

She nibbled a bit from each dish. Every time she tasted she looked upon me with a suspicious smile.

And how she slipped her sticks at the critical moment!

The sight amused me hugely.

"How dare I swallow raw fishes!" she said shrinking.

"What delight I taste in them!" I slammed back at her timidity.

Then I dipped a few cuts of the fishes into a porcelain soy pan for my mouth.

I even trampled into her fish-dish by and by.

She was literally terrified.

The feast was over. I said, "Go yukkuri! Honourable not-to-be-in-a-hurry!" I slid away.

I tied my white apron like a shop girl. I was glad that I did not forget to push a lead-pencil through my hair. I presented myself to Ada carrying a cigarette box.

"Will you buy tobacco for your lord?"

I spread the box before her.

"How much for one packet," she asked with the charming arrogance of a customer.

She was acting also.

"To-day is the memorial day of Lord Nono Sama. My sweet Oku San, allow me to make a reduction!"

Then we laughed.

13th—I created much noise in the Jap colony!

Why not?

Many brown men pause by my store and buy, simply because they can address a word or two to me.

They are silly, aren't they?

I announce that I am tired of their faces. I have never met one progressive-seeming Oriental since I landed. They are like a dry tree. Are their souls dying?

"Well, that's why, they have no girl," my uncle conclusioned.

He is so bright once in a while.

Why not make love with Meriken musume?

I said I would petition the Tokio government to transplant her women.

It may ruin the Japanese girl's name, was my afterthought, if they ship only the homely gang.

Lovely girl has no longing to sail over the ocean. She has plenty of chance to grow a flower bride at home.

I pity my native boys of this city.

"Jap! Jap!"

They are dashed with such exclamations from every corner.

As for me the sound of "Jap" is my taste, so I spray it in my writing.

I took up again my knitting work which I had commenced on the seas. Nothing could be more decent to fill up my leisure in the store.

My little neck fell, as I was intent on my stocking.

Some one spoke above my head: "How is business?"

"So, so!" I replied in businesslike reserve.

I lifted my face.

84

Oya, he was Mr. Consul.

"Will you sell me a cigar?"

"Things are becoming awfully high. Mine is a distinctly dear store. Do you know it, Mr. Consul?"

"I'm prepared to pay more at the beautiful girl's," he began to titter.

"General Arthur cigar has leaped one dollar higher since Monday, and— —"

"You don't mean it!" He mimicked a sudden alarm.

14th—O funny drunkard!

To-day one fellow established himself before my store. He fixed his amazing eyes on my face, and extended his hairy hand.

"Hel-lo, Japanese!" he stuttered.

He wanted to shake hands with me.

I lengthened my arm, and slapped his face. I withdrew directly within, and watched him from a hole.

"Ha, ha! She got mad—ha, ha, ha!"

He was in a tip-top state of mind.

"Let me help myself!"

He pilfered one cigar from the shelf. He struck a match. He bit the cigar.

"Good!" he muttered.

He tossed himself away with ludicrous dignity, singing:

"Pon pili, yon, pon, pon!"

"This is undeniably a tough place!" I exclaimed.

15th—Night has just arrived.

Only ten minutes ago a white-capped "Jim" (I overheard people calling him so) lighted a paper lantern labelled "Tomales." He is an eating-stand keeper across the street. The loafers passed. There was some time to watch the lazy parade. It was a blank hour of Saturday when he could puff a whiff of smoke.

The prankish songs ceased.

Even in Dupont Street I am given a page of dream.

The barkeeper of "Remember the Maine" called at my store.

"Remember the Maine?"

It is a name cheap as the grimness of a toothless woman.

Mr. Barkeeper had something to say, I imagined.

I offered a stem of cigarette.

"Do you ever hear a bloody cry at night?" he began his chapter, gathering a medley of gravity on his brow.

"Scream? No!"

"Never mind!"

He turned aside. I thought he was playing a threadbare artifice of a story-teller to tantalise my fancy.

"Tell me why!"

I knew I became his victim.

"I fear I do scare you."

"No! I never——" I leaned forward.

"To begin with——"

He stopped, looking around.

"Your kitchen—don't be scared—is close by a haunted room of a house on Pine Street. It's no story. A chorus girl lived—well, some five years ago—in that house with her step-mother. Just think! The old hen of sixty-five fell in love with her daughter's lover. Do you understand? She saw one morning the young fellow kissing her daughter. She went crazy. She shot him. Isn't it awful? The murderess leaned against the wall by your kitchen, and cried, 'I killed him!' I swear to you that it is all true. So, people say, a wail is heard at night from your side."

"Mah! Mah!" I breathed.

"That is all."

He retired heavily.

Do I believe it?

"No! No!" I denied.

But I was thickly swarmed by sickening air. How could I trust me in the kitchen!

I closed the store.

I pasted up a piece of paper whereon was written: "NO BUSINESS TO-NIGHT."

16th—I had a stomach-ache this morning. I couldn't rise.

86

The maid fetched me some toast and a cup of coffee.

I think it is very nice to eat in bed.

17th—Mrs. Wistaria and her husband returned from San Jose.

She lavished on me her thousand arigatos.

She said I sold sixty per cent more than on any previous week.

She wished me to condescend to accept a "meagre" fifteen dollars as a share of the profits.

I refused it.

18th—My letter to Miss Pine Leaf (who wept with me reading Keats' love-letters one mournful night) is as follows:

"Matsuba San:

'Hitofude mairase soro.

'I have the honour to present a brief writing.'

"Let me omit the shopworn form of Japanese letter-writing! Its redundant 'honourables' are more cheap than honourable.

"Satetoya!

"Shall I begin my letter with a deep bow?

"Bow?

"I use it occasionally before Meriken San for sport's sake. But it is degenerating, in my opinion, to comic opera, like the tortoise-shell-framed spectacles of a Chinese doctor.

"Now I address you with a thousand kisses.

"The kiss is the thing to begin with for up-to-date girls.

"It is useful, as a poem is useful in filling up space in magazine-making. Woman—even a loftily learned American woman—cannot be ready always with her rhetoric of expression. The kiss comes to her relief in the crisis whenever she fails in speech.

"The kiss is everything.

"The Jap girl is intimate with the art of crying.

"A kiss is as eloquent as a tear.

"I suppose the cleverness of American woman is graded by the way she handles it. It strikes me that every white girl is perfectly at home with it.

"She is awfully bright.

"You wonder why she is so?

"There is one reason that I can tell you. It is because she has a serious job to pick out her husband herself. I don't think it is fair to blame her growing insipid after marriage. Every one feels tired when a weighty work is done. What would be her doom if she were stupid? An old maid is such a sad sight, like a broken clock, or a cradle after baby's death. Isn't it dreadful to have nothing to rejoice in but a customary tea or books? Literary critic is one occupation left for her. Worse than death!

"I am pained to state that our brown sisters are extremely behind time.

("There are lots of exceptions, of course, like honourable you and Miss M. G.)

"I am talking of common Jap musumes.

"Naturally so.

"They are like those waiting at the station for the next train. They have only to doze and wait for the footsteps of a matchmaker with a young man.

"I am grateful to the Nippon government for stimulating education in women.

"But I advise her to imprison all the matchmakers. Then the girls will wake up at once, like one who has everything on her back after papa's passing.

"That is one process to brighten them, I think.

"Am I not logical?

"Your last tegami questioned me whether the American lady was charming.

"Are you attentive to western sea painting?

"How does it impress you when you are close by it? Only a jumble of paint, isn't it? So with Meriken woman!

88

"You should be off half a dozen steps to estimate her beautiful captivation. You would be horrified, otherwise, by her hairy skin.

"I love her.

"She has no headache like the Japs. (By the way, I will call Japan, hereafter, the country of headache.) She lives in a comedy.

"Nothing turns bad in Amerikey.

"'Tragedy To Be a Woman,' could only be seen on a fiction thrown in a moth-trodden second-hand store.

"Police never bother.

"Such a deliverance!

"I am delighted with my Meriken Kenbutsu.

"Sayonara!

Yours,
"Morning Glory"

19th—I forced Uncle to swear to me that he would overlook everything I did, in consideration of my great service in darning his socks.

I peeled off my shoes to begin with.

I sat like a Turk.

"Why do you frown like an Oni in hell?" I acidified my smile. I held my needle and thread suspended in the air, while I said: "What is a Trust?"

"Be quiet!" he exclaimed.

He didn't even glance at me, being engaged in writing in the other nook.

"Uncle, your hair ought to be curled. I will step in to-morrow morning, and turn it up before you awake. What do you think, Uncle? Oji San!"

"Morning Glory San!"

He emitted a growl of satanic despotism, and soon resumed his work gracefully.

I thought what a scandal if he were penning a love letter to Mrs. Schuyler, junior.

89

I rose. I approached him with secret step. I fell on him from his massy back and cried:

"What are you scribbling?"

Erai, my honourable uncle!

He was translating Gibbon's "History of Rome."

I was stunned from the shame of taking him to be in such a wretched line even in fancy.

I vowed to myself—with three low bows—to take perfect care of my noble worker.

Then I gave him my sweet smile.

"Uncle, let me fix something more! Haven't you anything? Tear your shirt or pull off the buttons, then!"

20th—Already I could suck from the agile air the flavour of spring upon the lawn.

I was roving by the rose-bushes along the street with scissors.

A gentleman passed by me. How sluggish his shoes sounded! He stopped, waving his old-scented smile, and addressed me:

"Good morning, young lady!"

"Ohayo!"

"I perceive that you are Japanese."

"Yes, sir!"

He stepped nearer to me. I took a peep at the Bible under his arm.

"Are you a Christian?" he lowered his tone.

"Don't you read the Gospel?" his voice rose higher.

"Don't you attend church?" his sound grew higher still.

"I love to be shocked. I couldn't sustain myself against a bore. Church? It's too sleepy, don't you know? I have remarked that God is with me without any sort of prayer, if I trace the path of righteousness. A minister is only a meddling grandmamma to my mind. If I ever build my ideal city, two things shall not be tolerated. One is a lawyer's office and the other is a church. Church, sir! May I present you with one rose?"

I raised me to place it in his coat.

"Here's a letter for you, Morning Glory!"

I was rescued by my uncle. How angelic his voice rang!

"I'm sorry, I'm much occupied this very morning," I said, bowing slightly.

I pushed myself within the door.

Poor preacher!

21st—My answer to Oscar is as follows:

"Dear Honourable Mr. Ellis:

"Let me begin in respectable fashion!

"A Jap girl is awfully formal.

"Do you know, Mr. Ellis, whom you are addressing?

"I am an Oriental.

"Nippon daughters believe 'ev'rithin' a gentleman mentions.

"They have been fooled enough, I should declare, in American fiction. Oscar—no, Mr. Ellis—don't let me earn the anecdote that I drifted to Ameriky to be toyed with! My ancestor did a harakiri. I am pretty sure I have, then, to kill myself.

"Don't recite again your honourable confession of love!

"It made me cry.

"My dark face with drenched eyes will degrade me to a hired Chinese 'crying woman.'

"Your narration was dramatic.

"Your cleverness is the most lamentable thing about you. Woman used to love a bright fellow many years ago. Do you know that the modern girl woos a stupid man?

"Please, don't repeat again such an adjective as 'heavenly' for my face! No one utters the word 'heaven' except in swearing. Even ministers juggle with it for a jest in church, I suppose. My face isn't heavenly at all. You know it, don't you?

"You amused me, however, when you told how you had pillaged my picture from Mother Schuyler's room to put in your own, feigning that it needed to be retouched.

91

"Poor Mother Schuyler!

"If she knew your secret!

"Frankly, I fear that such a gentleman as you does commit forgery always. Have you no consanguinity with a convict?

"O such a wretched boy!

"The saddest thing about a woman is that she is glad to fall in love with the worthless.

"Do I love you?

"Give me time to reply to the question!

"Everything is tardy with a Japanese. I was educated by slowness; I bow one dozen times before I speak.

"O Oscar, you got to think of my side a little bit!

"Every girl claims that she has half a population as adorers in her pocket handkerchief.

"You are the only one young American I ever met.

"If I accept your love, I am afraid one may satirise my destitution.

"You'll write me soon, won't you?

"*Yours, M. G.*

"P.S.—I wish I could show you how charmingly I smoke. I learned the art recently. I tap the cigarette with my middle finger to knock the ashes off. It is delightful to heap a hill of ashes on the table edge. When I puff, finding no word after 'And—' the smoke seems to be speaking for me.

"But I assure you that I smoked only before my uncle.

"I was a pretty naughty girl at home, but I flatter myself that I can easily be classed among the best in this country.

"White women behave terribly, you know."

22nd—I passed the afternoon at Mrs. Consul's. She gave me her "favourite" discourse on Walt Whitman.

I delivered to my uncle what I had learned.

"No newness in it. It is what dear John Burroughs or Mr. Stedman said."

He overturned my castle with one blow, and lit his cigar with a victorious air.

I was enraged.

"Yes, yes, eraiwa! Oriental gentleman knows everything we poor women know," I said.

I sulkily drew away to my room with Mr. Whitman's fat book, that I borrowed from Mrs. Consul.

23rd—A letter from my father arrived.

"O Papa, please don't! I am tired of such a dirty conference." I scoffed.

I tore the paper into shreds.

"What a sullen lady! What did Otto San write? Marriage proposal, I reckon!" my uncle intruded.

"Papa threatened me with a list of suitors. He cried, 'Chance, chance!' like the gate-man of an ennichi show. Pray grant me for once in my life, Uncle, to say: 'The marriage lottery go to the dogs!' How many Jap girls kill themselves from the burden of such a glued union, do you suppose?"

"Then, 'free marriage'?"

"Of course!"

"It's very beautiful, Miss Morning Glory."

"Why not?"

"You are Japanese, aren't you?"

"Did you ever think I was a Meriken jin?"

"Well, then, how did you come to know young men in a country where familiarity with one is regarded as a crime for a girl?"

"Things all wrong in Nippon, Uncle!"

"I am sorry you were born a Jap."

"I'll never go back to Japan, I think. The dictionary for Jap girls comprises no such word as 'No.' But you must remember, Uncle, I have the capital 'No' in my head. I am a revolutionist," I proclaimed.

Then I thought much of my dear Oscar.

93

24th—My worthy labourer upon Gibbon's work sat before the table for some hours.

I stood behind him and dropped the fluid from a bottle on his head.

"Cold! What are you doing, my little romp?" He looked up in a fright.

"No harm, Uncle! It is only a remedy. Your hair is growing so thin. Do you know it? I think it a shame to appear in Greater New York with a bald gentleman."

I bought the bottle this morning.

25th—A bamboo table in my room reminded me of a take bush in the neighbouring churchyard of my Tokio home.

(I cannot sound Meriken jin's curiosity in prizing such a cheap thing. The bamboo was painted. The cross nails glared from everywhere. I never saw such a Jap work in Nippon.)

Dear take, O bamboo bush!

How I used to laugh, breaking the dreams of sparrows by wriggling the bush!

I was so ungoverned.

If I could be a grammar school girl again!

I secured a reader at a bookstall. My mind was made up to present myself in the Lincoln night school and mingle with the girls in "SEE THE BOY AND THE DOG!"

What fun!

I went to see the stooping principal. His tarnished frock-coat—I fancied he was an old bachelor, as one button was off—was just the thing for such a rôle.

I seemed to him a regular nenne of thirteen.

He was heartily pleased with my greediness for learning English.

Poor soul!

He ushered me into the class for which I had brought the book.

It was the hour for composition. "Ocean," the subject.

When I was seated, the girl next me winked charmingly. She threw me a note within a minute, to which I promptly replied, "Morning Glory." My note was answered "Miss Madge, 340

94

Mission Street." I wrote her, "May I call on you to-morrow?" for which she wrote, "As you please."

I was placed on the dangerous verge of clapping Byron's poem into my "Ocean." I manufactured one dozen of spelling errors.

"You should belong to some higher class. Take this slip to the principal!" the teacher said. "You have an imagination." She wiped her spectacles slowly.

I left the room remarking, "Because I am a Japanese."

I slipped away from the school altogether.

"One experience is plenty," I declared.

26th—I went to Mission Street to call on Madge.

From both sides of the street peeped the famous Jewish noses. The second-hand clothing shops parade. How droll to see those noses shrivelling like a lobster!

Madge's father owns a despicable restaurant with only four eating tables. Mamma cooks, while she sits on the counter.

When I appeared, she shot out, greeting me: "Hello, Morning Glory!"

"Awfully glad to see you! I have come to help you, haven't I?"

I was ready to strip off my jacket and wind myself in her apron.

Her papa was dumbfounded by my sudden action.

The outside board with the bill of fare was scraped out by this morning's rain. It looked as miserable as an Italian vegetable wagon under the rain.

My first work was to rewrite it.

I saw a Jew at a neighbouring door striving with one about the value of pants. A shoemaker's "pan, pan" hammered on my head from the opposite house.

Mission Street is the street of horse-dung.

When my job was over, an honourable Mr. Wagon Driver leaped in, bidding me serve some soup.

I ran into the kitchen to fetch it.

I spilled it on the table.

"That's all right, honey!" he said in patronising aloofness, and pierced my face with his gummy red eyes.

O Kowaya! Shocking!

I put one five-dollar piece of gold on Madge's palm when I left her.

Because her shoes were heelless.

Pity the musume!

27th—I bought one book, being captivated by its title. Isn't "When Knighthood was in Flower" beautifully chivalrous?

I have remarked that every Imperial cruiser anchors at an isle close by Loo Choo, just on account of the enticement in the name "Come and See."

I found in my trunk an introduction to Miss Rose by my professor friend of Tokio 'versity.

Miss Rose?

My imagination started to move like a watch. I fancied she should be nineteen, since she was a Miss. No Rose girl can be homely.

I went to see her.

Alas!

She was a lady like a beer-barrel. Her finger-nails were black.

I left her like a miner stepping out of a gold mountain with empty hands.

I wonder why the mayor didn't object to letting an ugly woman be crowned with a pretty name.

Fifty-years-old Miss Rose!

Now I fear to read Mr. Major's book.

28th—The following is my letter to Mr. Oscar:

"Oscar San! Ellis San!

"I never liked your profession, simply because it is too beautiful.

"I don't see why you cannot transfer to some other business.

"I have been ever so much fascinated with odd sorts of manual work. If I were a gentleman, I would very likely pursue the calling of grave-digger or sea-diver.

96

"Yesterday I passed by some labourers breaking massive stones. They lifted their hammers (O Oscar, look at their muscles!) and knocked them down to the sound of 'Sara bagun!' They jerked the 'sara bagun,' Oscar. Does it mean 'ready?' Mrs. Willis' Century dictionary must be imperfect, since it does not contain such a word. Am I mis-spelling?

"Suppose I marry one of those!

"He will return home awfully tired. He will naturally doze after dinner. When his smoking pipe has slipped from his lips and burned my best tablecloth, isn't it possible that I will be mad?... I startled him, pulling his hair ever so hard. Now you must think that he grew mad also. He seized my arm, and beat me. O Oscar, he beat me surely!... Then he will repent his conduct, and kneel by my side, begging my forgiveness. He will say, 'My dear sweet wife—'

"Do you know how interesting it is to be beaten by a husband?

"I well-nigh fixed my mind never to affiance with a man too genteel to hit me.

"Woman is a revolting little bit of thing.

"If you say 'Yes,' I am quite ready to slam my 'No!'

"Oscar San!

"I am afraid that you are too amiable.

"What you have to do for your next missive is to collect every kind of dreadful adjectives from your dictionary, and throw them in.

"You know what to do when I get angry, don't you?

"Ellis San!

"You are too handsome.

"I am fond of a comely face as anybody else.

"But I fancy often how it would be if I fell in love with a deformity.

"People would laugh at me doubtless. But how dramatic it would be when I proclaimed, 'Because I love him!'

"What a romantic phrase that is!

"Can't you deform yourself?

"Sayonara,

"With a thousand bows,

"M. G.

"P.S.—My letter never finishes without a P.S.

"Isn't that awful?

"My uncle asked me whom I was corresponding with. I mentioned 'Olive.'

"Old man is jealous always.

"So you got to counterfeit your sister's penmanship for your envelope."

29th—I drank the last drop of my coffee.

"Oji San, when shall we go to New York?" I said, pillowing my face on my hands on the breakfast table.

"As soon as spring begins to flicker in the East, my little woman! It's snow and snow there at present."

"I love snow, Uncle."

"Old gentleman can't bear tyrannical cold, Morning Glory."

"Don't you notice how tired I am of Frisco? Aren't you tired?"

"Yes—frankly!"

"Why don't you then contrive some novel diversion to pass a month?"

"I've a fancy, but——"

"What is it?"

"It may not strike you as romantic."

"Tell me!"

"I am known to one poet who dreams and erects a stone wall on the hillside. He is unlike another. His garden and cottage are open to everybody. I ever incline to loaf in an irregular puff of odour from his acacia trees. If you lean towards a poetical life, I have no hesitation in seeing him to make an arrangement."

"Great Uncle, it's romantic! Is he married?"

"Why?"

"Because a poet is not one woman's property, but universal. My ideal poet is melancholy. Fat poet is ridiculous. Happy poet isn't of the highest order. Tennyson? I wish his life had been more hard up. I suppose your friend-poet won't mind if I sleep all day. Is he particular about the dinner time? Does he look up to the stars every night? Does he wash his shirt once in a while?"

"Stop!"

Then I asked respectably:

"Is the sight from there beautiful?"

"Wonderful! The only place where you can breathe the air of divinity!"

"Very well, Uncle. We will settle there, and hasten to become poets."

"It wouldn't be a bad idea, I say, to start again with your honourable 'Lotos Eaters!'"

"'Paradise Lost' shall be my next subject."

"If nobody publishes it?"

"I will present it solemnly to our Empress. She is a poetess, you know."

My uncle went to see Mr. Poet.

30th—Uncle said that the poet said: "You are welcome, sir. The cottage for your young lady lies by one willow tree. The waters, the air, the grand view, are God's. It costs a wee bit of money to provide the best coffee. I tell you that my claret is superb. You shall be my guest as long as you please. Present my love to Miss Morning Glory! Everything will be ready when you come."

"Isn't he adorable?" I ejaculated.

I stirred my trunk, and sifted out the things needful for my adventure.

31st—To-morrow!

The Heights, Feb. 1st

Let me recline heart-to-heart on the breast of Mother Nature!

Let me retreat to a hillside not far from the city, yet verily near to God! Let me go to my poet abode!

We abandoned the Fruitvale car at the hill-foot.

My uncle picked out our destination from the speckles in the distance.

The breeze (how heavenly is a country breeze!) enticed my soul—a Jap girl also is provided with some soul—into "Far-Beyond."

"I feel myself another girl, Uncle."

"How?"

"I'm a poet already. The poet without poem is greater, don't you know?"

We climbed the hill slowly. Every step enlarged the spectacle.

When we attained to one wildly well-kept garden, the whole bay of the Golden Gate stretched before us. A thousand villages knelt humbly like vassals.

I saw a tiny gate with the sign:

"Fruit Grower."

An old gentleman appeared from a cottage, singing.

"Ah, take the Cash, and let the Credit go,
Nor heed the rumble of a distant Drum!"

"Poet!" Uncle whispered.

Let me now examine him!

What lengthy hair he wore!

It didn't annoy me, however, because he stamped himself on my mind as if he were an ancient statue. I imagined him a type of mediæval squire. I thought of him truly as one metamorphosed from the frontispiece of a wholly forgotten volume in a cobwebbed recess of a library.

His courteous voice was simply dignified.

"Nature never hurries. God commands you every happiness and all repose. Here's your little home, my gentle lady! I am at your service any time. I hope you will find it comfortable."

He set me at the "Willow Cottage."

He slipped gracefully away.

There was some time before I heard his "kotsu kotsu" on my door.

I opened it.

"Greeting from the host!" Mr. Heine offered me a tuft of brisk roses.

Heine was the poet's name.

How loving!

I buried myself in the thought of straying to a fairy isle, and being accepted romantically by the dwellers.

I suspected that I was dreaming.

"Arcadia!" I exclaimed, when the poet announced that supper would be prepared within half an hour.

I spied him through the window, gathering the loppings of trees and leaves. He made a camp-fire. Its soft smoke surged into the sky. Oh, smell it!

How fascinating is the Poet's life!

I ran out, crying:

"Pray, make me useful!"

2nd—Dream and reality are not marked here by different badges. They waltz round. Dear poet home!

Was it in my dream that I heard the tinkle of bells?

I thought something was going on.

I parted from the bed. I pushed out my face from the window.

Look at the procession of cows!

I have read much of them, but I admit that it was my first occasion to admire them. I am a trivial Jap, only acquainted with cherry blossoms and lanterns. How I wished to knot the bells round my waist, and whisk down the path by the violets!

"Lover's lane!"

It should be the title for that path, I thought, if I were Mr. Poet.

I finished my toilet. I leaped out upon the grasses smiling up to the sunlight.

I congratulated myself on my new life.

Then I found my uncle sitting by the camp-fire.

"Ohayo!" I said, filling the seat on another side.

I remember one Japanese essay, "The Poetry of a Tea Kettle." Indeed! The kettle was a singer. Its melody was far-reaching. It was like a harp of pine leaves fingered by the zephyr.

I faced up, and saw my poet moving down from the lily pond. Two frogs in his hand.

"Frogs?" I cried.

"They will complete our table. How did you sleep, my lady?"

"Splendid!"

"Do you love the country?"

"I begin to taste a greater joy in Nature."

"I'm happy to hear it, my dear. My life is like the life of a bird. I awake when the sun rises. I lay me in the bed at the bird's dipping into its nest. God made the night for keeping quiet. That is better than prayer itself. I light neither lamp nor candle. I presume that every young lady has certain secret work at night. Let me offer you a few candles!"

We ate breakfast from the table by the fire.

Frogs supplied a special dish.

I couldn't touch it, thinking of the songs of frogs that I had heard all the night long.

Such a song! It was the muddy-booted song of the countryside. No valuable quality in it, of course. But I should say that they tried the best they could.

Poor Messrs. Frog!

I fancied the leg in my dish was that of one who volunteered to sing my lullaby.

I almost cried in grief.

The poet was ready to wash the dishes. I was quick to snatch his job. My uncle wiped them.

Stupid uncle!

He broke two dishes.

I collected the bones of the frogs, and buried them. On the stone above them I wrote with a pencil:

"Tomb of Unknown Singers."

What time was it when we were done with our breakfast?

I couldn't tell.

The first thing I did yesterday was to stop the tick-tack of my watch, and hide it in the lowest drawer.

The watch is a nuisance since I am thrown in The Garden of Eternity.

3rd—I searched for a pen and ink in my Willow Cottage.

Nothing like those.

Foxy Poet!

He hid them from view, I fancied, in the opinion that playing with them for a girl is more jeopardous than swallowing needles.

I say that letter-writing—particularly a decent love letter, if there is one—isn't half so grave a crime as rhyming.

I was spraying some water on a rose by the gate, when I caught sight of a white quill by my shoes.

"This will serve me perfectly," I said.

I had not one thing with any tooth except my comb. (Comb? Luckily I have not lost it Ara, ma, my hairpins! Five of them vanished from my head while I was springing amid the rocks. By and by the stems of acacia leaves shall be used in their places. Don't you know this is quite a remote spot from civilisation?) A kitchen knife shaped my quill as a pen.

Now only ink!

I begged Uncle to run down three miles to fetch one bottle.

4th—We went to "breathe the song of the forest."

The forest laces the poet's canyon.

(By the way, poet's ground spreads over one hundred and fifty acres. Does he pay taxes?)

We climbed the "Road to the Milky Way." I beseech your forgiveness, it was merely the name I wished for the path to the poet's hilltop. I felt as if I were hurrying to the "Sermon on the Mount." You would hardly believe Morning Glory if she said that sublimity vibrated in her soul, because she was just a little Oriental. How grand! We faced toward the Gate of the Pacific Ocean. We were still. Why? Because we were thinking the same thing.

We traversed the poet's graveyard.

How romantic to put up a tombstone while living!

103

How romantic to lie in the ecstasy of a marvellous view! We could be nearer the stars here.

We stepped down to the canyon.

The poet said solemnly:

"Lady and gentleman, this is a holy place where you can pray heartily."

My uncle started to drone Bryant's hymn:

"The groves were God's first temples."

"Did you ever read Thanatopsis, my dear?" Mr. Heine asked.

"Yes, sir!"

"It's a noble piece. So many thousand Asiatics converted every year to the English alphabet. Wonderful!" he soliloquised.

We seated ourselves by a brook.

"Such a lesson in Nature! We endeavour to transcribe, but fail," he sighed, looking on the trees.

Then he turned to me questioning:

"Do you hear the silent song of the forest?"

I nodded.

"Silence! Silence!" he muttered.

We walked among the trees. We came back to the same hilltop, when the large red ball of the sun sank heavily from the Gate.

"Bye-bye!" I shook my handkerchief.

The playful breeze carried it away. It glimmered like a silvery inspiration. Who knows how far it sailed?

I thought a huge statue of the Muse bidding sayonara to the dying sun would be the fitting ornamentation for these Heights. Countless numbers of people would look upon it from the valley. It would be a salvation, if they could bind themselves with Poesy by its noble figure. There was no question it would be more effective than a thousand pages of poem.

"I have no coin to build it," the poet said, in dear openness.

"Let me present it by and by!"

"When?"

"When? It must be after I get married to a rich philanthropist."

We laughed.

We rolled down the hill in the purple fragrance of evening. The evening was sweet like a legend.

5th—I wrote a letter to the artist:

"My sweet Oscar:

"You will love no more your Morning Glory, I am certain, when you are informed how she looks nowadays.

"She inclines against a willow trunk by her cottage. Were you ever acquainted with the great repose of a poetess? Her eyes flash in divine sarcasm. She will shoot them down to the mortal domain (she lives on the mountain), while she murmurs in tragical accents: 'I pity you, ant-mortals!'

"Isn't she shocking?

"Oscar, I have withdrawn to the Heights, and am prying into the Incomprehensible of Nature with Mr. Heine.

"He is unique.

"I take it upon me to say that he is a great poet. Because, in the first place, he never asked me yet, 'Do poems pay in Japan?'

"It's such a trying work for an old man like him to pose as a poet all the time.

"Poet is a sensitive creation. He fancies, I think, the whole world is staring at him. Poor Poet! He keeps up, and tries to be picturesque as he can.

"I am grieved to state, however, that his picturesqueness frequently drops into silliness.

"The absurd thing is that even my uncle takes a part in his farce.

"We had no meat to bite yesterday.

"The poet had no shot left for his gun.

"What did he plan, do you imagine?

"He went up the hill, shouldering his pick. My uncle retainered him with a spade.

"'We will soon bring back a squirrel which we will dig out, Miss Morning Glory,' the poet said.

"Could you ever suppose, Oscar, that any animal except an invalid (an animal who has four feet at that, instead of two like my venerable gentlemen) could permit itself to be so slow like them?

"I laughed till my side ached.

"Funny old men!

"Every sort of sweat fell from their brows when they dragged their fatigued feet home not accompanied by even one inch of any animal tail.

"'I have never heard yet, Mr. Poet, of a squirrel turned to turnip,' I gibed.

"I dread old age, because it makes woman inquisitive, and man silly. Inquisitiveness is tasteless like wax, while silliness is helpless, like a fish on the sand.

"I fear you are silly already, when you say that you sat up late looking at my picture.

"Sat up late?

"What will you do if your mamma thinks you can't sleep from hard drink when you yawn continually at the table?

"Please, don't do it again!

"Step to your bed at half-past six as I do!

"Are you sure that my picture approved your act?

"I guess it shrugged its shoulders from contempt, the delicious moment of blushing being passed.

"If my picture is so precious, I advise you to alter it to ashes. You will take two spoonfuls of the ashes every morning. I am sure, then, your soul will be saved.

"O my darling, I love you!

"*I am your*
"*Little Jap Girl*

"P.S.—This letter was written by my duck-quill. My new invention, you know.

106

"My handwriting is clumsy enough, I suppose, to sell as high as any ancient author's autograph.

"Sayonara!"

6th—O poppy, beloved harbinger of California spring!

I "hung on the honourable eyes" of a poppy by my door. Its quaking cup burnt in love (for a meadow-lark perhaps).

"Let me feed you, my new friend!" I said, and brought out a cupful of water.

I moistened it.

A golden flake of the sun-ray came down to it. It smiled, daintily thanking me for my humble treat.

I stared at it, slowly fabricating a fable of its love affair, when the breeze sent me a dreamy song.

The song was old-fashioned, like the afternoon snore of a water-wheel.

I plunged into the song, not knowing who was the singer.

"Ara, ara, Grandmamma's song!" I exclaimed.

She is the aged mother of our poet. She is within the rim of ninety. I suspected her of having discovered the "Elixir for Preserving Eternal Girlhood." You cannot help esteeming her a philosopher when you are told that she has visited San Francisco only twice in ten years. I have no bit of doubt that she would die if you were to rob her of the sight of her flower garden and one stout scrap-book about her son's poems. They work a miracle. What a mystery is human life!

I say that I'm touched by superstition.

I have read of a villainous fox who masquerades in the shape of an old woman.

My wretched fantasy about Mrs. Heine passed, when I heard that no fox resided in the hill.

She is such a dear grandma.

She has no hostile grimace against age. She welcomes it. Her wrinkles are all her beauty. Natural ripening in age is but another form of girlhood.

She is happy as a sparrow.

(Sparrow never forgets, it is said in Nippon, to dance in its hundredth year.)

She hoes round her garden. Her vanity is to make her table rich with her own potatoes and roses.

She lives alone by herself in a cottage some hundred steps from mine.

Did you ever taste her cooking?

"Good morning, Mrs. Heine!" I said.

"Come in!"

She showed herself, extending her large hands. They were damp. I thought she was employing herself in washing.

Is there any sweeter occupation than service to an old lady?

"Let me help you!"

I carried out a bucket to a spring in the backyard.

I brimmed it with the waters. It was so weighty. A naughty stone bounced under my heel. I was thrown down like a toy.

Alas!

My bucket was upset over my skirt.

I had made myself a specimen of misery. "O grandma, it's raining awfully outside!" I cried.

7th—To-day I was the chef, while my uncle was second cook.

I placed a heroic iron pot over the camp-fire I dropped a lump of beef in, and afterward the mass of potatoes, carrots, and onions. Mr. Poet's directions were that they should boil for two hours.

Mr. Heine intruded, saying that he would like to season them himself.

"Longfellow, Lowell—they all loved high seasoning as I," he said, snatching a pepper-box from my hand.

He kept tapping the bottom of the box, when the cover fell into the pot.

Oya!

The red pepper garmented the whole thing.

"Go, Mr. Poet! Why don't you mind your own business? You are butler to-day." I spoke in rough sweetness, and drove him away.

108

He began to place a linen cloth on the table, while I dipped up all the pepper. He picked up one dozen pebbles to weight the tablecloth. The first thing he put on the table was his claret bottle. How could he lose it from sight! When he said that everything was in place, he had forgotten the knives and forks. Dear old poet!

We sat at the table under the wild rose bushes.

Mr. Heine read aloud the following menu:

"Perfume of Omar's Rose
Water of Jordan River
Mother Love Broth
Meat of Wisdom
Potatoes of Simplicity
Passion Carrot
Onion of Wit
Dream Coffee.

Dessert

Typical Tokio Smile of Miss Morning Glory."

My grandmamma was our guest.

"Mother, you talk too much always. Remember, this is a sacred service. Silence helps your digestion. Eat slowly, think something higher, and be content!" Poet said.

We smelled the "Perfume of Omar's Rose," and wet our lips with the "Water of Jordan River."

The broth was served.

Everybody choked with its pungent fire.

Poor Mrs. Heine!

She was showering her tear-beans.

"This is perfectly seasoned. Send up your bowl again, ladies and gentlemen!"

Mr. Poet's performance was beautifully buffoonish.

We finished our meat and vegetables.

I smiled lightly, and said: "Are you ready for the Tokio smile?"

"Just ten minutes yet, my dear!" The poet smoothed such a lengthy gray beard.

I winked to Grandma. We looked upon him slyly.

8th—The poet was hoeing in his vegetable garden.

His attire was theatrical.

His red crape sash laxly surrounding his trousers lacked, I am sorry to say, a large Japanese tobacco bag. The cap with gay ribbons was like one of Li Hung Chang's. His back carried a bearskin, inside of which some slovenly yellow silk flapped down.

How tall he was!

"Please, don't dig over there, Mr. Heine, because I buried my poem there," I said.

"What poem, my lady?" he asked.

"The poem to be read at the unveiling of my statue of the Muse on your mountain top, which may occur possibly within five years. The opening lines sound thus:

> 'Victor of Life and Song,
> O Muse of golden grace!'"

"That's great! Why did you bury it?"

"Don't you bury your poems? The best poems are those not published. The very best are those not written. Dante Gabriel Rosetti buried his 'House of Life,' because they were not for a gaping millionaire's wife, but only for his own little wife. But his greatness was ruined when he dug them up and sold them. Poor poet! What all the poets ought to do, I think, is to bury their poems in a potato garden. What a shame even the poets have to eat once in a while! They should wait till the potatoes grow, and then sell them in a vegetable stand, calling 'Poetical Potatoes!' Do you sell your poems, Mr. Heine?"

"Yes."

"Aren't you making your living with your fruits?"

"I never sell them, my dear."

"What do you do?"

"I give them to needy persons. But I was obliged, last year, to hang up a sign, 'No Fruit Lover is Wanted.' I told an Oakland minister to come up and eat some plums. He brought his wife and children, even his grand-mother. They shouldered away every bit of fruit from half a dozen trees. Next day so many people trampled in with an introduction from the minister."

"Such a minister! I see no use to have the sign, 'Fruit Grower,' if you don't sell."

"Well, my dear lady, God will be merciful to let me use it in place of 'Poem Manufacturer!'"

My uncle announced that tea was boiled.

We left the garden.

9th—The fogs held possession of our world, like the darkness of night.

Where did they invade from?

Pacific Ocean?

Our hillside cottages looked like a tottering ship having no hope for any haven.

Tremendous sight!

I planted me on the hilltop. My mind merged in Japanese mythology. I felt as if I were the first goddess, Izanagi, standing on the "Floating Bridge of Heaven," before the creation.

The divine ghastliness bit my little soul.

I couldn't stand against it. I crept down like a mouse.

The poet said he was preparing a lecture. Its title was "Not in Books."

He in his bed—there he passes every forenoon—was reciting his song.

The words leapt like a leaping sword:

"Sail on! Sail! Sail on! And on!"

I threw a bunch of roses over to his bed as an admirer does to a star.

Then I clapped my hands.

111

"Pan, pan! Pan, pan!"

10th—I went up the hill to gather mushrooms and watercresses.

I filled a huge basket with them.

I carried it down on my shoulder in Chinese laundry style. I paused every twenty steps.

I slipped within the gate of Mrs. Heine's back garden.

"Mush—rooms! Water—cresses!" I called boisterously.

"My dear girl!" Grandma smiled out from her door.

"Keep your hands off, please! They are things for sale. To-day they are uncommonly cheap. Will you buy them?"

"How much do you charge?"

"Two thousand words of the story about your illustrious son's life."

"What a funny vendor!"

"Tell me something about him! I'm ready to leave you the whole business."

"Shall I narrate to you how he started to write?"

"How interesting!" I ejaculated.

"Let me see your things first!" she said, tugging the basket nearer.

"My dear child, they aren't watercresses, but baby weeds. I don't consider they are legitimate mushrooms, either."

She turned upon me with compassionate objection.

"Oya, oya, you don't say so!" I exclaimed. "Then, no story, Grandma?" I looked up meekly.

11th—We had sipped our supper tea some time ago.

A band from the bay sent up irregularly the melody of the love and prowess of dear mariners.

The white moon rose.

I sat alone on my front step, and watched tenderly by the poppy.

My darling Miss Poppy shook herself prettily, as if she uttered a sweet word out of her heart. I imagined every sort of speech that may come from such a tiny bit of flower.

112

"Sodah, she said that she loved me!" I murmured.
I made a little letter.

"Miss Poppy:
"I love you too.
"Yours,
"Morning Glory."

I rolled it to a ball. I dropt it in her cup.
The moon turned gold. The evening odour filled the air.
Look!
She was folding her cup, pressing my missive to her breast.
There was no question that she understood.
Dearest friend!
Was it silly that I cried?

12th—The poet left the Heights to exchange his MS. for a gallon of whiskey.

He carried a demijohn, which was as apt to him as a baby to a woman.

I volunteered to clean his holy grotto.

The little cottage brought me a thought of one Jap sage who lived by choice in a ten-foot square mountain hut. The venerable Mr. Chomei Kamo wrote his immortal "Ten-Foot Square Record." A bureau, a bed, and one easy chair—everything in the poet's abode inspires repose—occupy every bit of space in Mr. Heine's cottage. The wooden roof is sound enough against a storm. A fountain is close by his door. Whenever you desire, you may turn its screw and hear the soft melody of rain.

That's plenty. What else do you covet?

The closetlessness of his cottage is a symbol of his secretlessness. How enviable is an open-hearted gentleman! Woman can never tarry a day in a house without a closet.

He never closes his door through the year.

A piece of wire is added to his entrance at night. He would say that that will keep out the tread of a dog and a newspaper reporter.

Not even one book.

113

He would read the history written on the brow of a star, he will say if I ask him why.

Every side was patched by pictures and a medley of paper clippings. Is there anything sweeter to muse upon than personal knick-nacks?

O such a dust!

I swept it.

But I thought philosophically afterward, why should people be so fussy with the dust, when things are but another form of dust. What a far-away smell the dust had! What an ancient colour!

I observed on the wall an odd coat and boots that dear old Santa Claus might have lost.

"Klondyke costume!" I exclaimed.

I undressed myself, and tried them on.

When I was ready to put on a fur cap, Mrs. Heine wandered down, calling me.

"Morning Glory! Morning Glory!"

I trembled in deadly fear.

I hid me promptly by the bureau, under the bed. I shut my eyes, praying:

"Namu Daijingu, don't let her find me!"

13th—Last midnight (O voicelessness of the hillside yonaka!) I woke up. The moon peeped into my sitting-room. She laid a square looking-glass on the floor.

I abandoned my bed, and sat by the glass.

I spread on it the letter from my sweetheart.

I read it over and over, till I couldn't read any more, the moon being kidnapped by the cloud-highwayman.

"O Oscar!"

I cried in the darkness.

I could not slumber all the night, on account of my thought of him.

A letter was written to him to-day.

Nature and love! I am now living with them.

14th—I elaborated a nosegay.

114

The poet and uncle dignified themselves in frock-coats.

The coming of the coffin was slow.

Mr. Poet had proffered his own graveyard to let an unknown poet lodge there. "Is it because you want some one to greet you when you die?" I said in laughter.

I seated myself by a creek.

I entered involuntarily into the riddle of Life and Death.

The water under my feet rolled down, positively not knowing why nor whence. The wind passed, "willy-nilly blowing." I wondered whither it went. Mr. Omar is unquestionably a true poet. The petals of a rose before me fell.

I murmured:

> "Each Morn a thousand Roses brings, you say;
> Yes, but where leaves the Rose of Yesterday?"

I was crying in sadness when the coffin arrived.

Mr. Heine and my uncle lifted it by either edge. The neighbouring farmers and two sardonically cool gentlemen from the undertaker's aided them. The jaw-fallen papa of the dead carried all the posies.

And Miss Morning Glory (who is the belle of Tokio) shouldered a bench for the purpose of sustaining the coffin when they were tired.

The hill is precipitous.

The gentlemen stopped numberless times, before they stationed themselves on the top.

The grave was hollowed behind Mr. Poet's monument. They sank the coffin.

What a tremor of silence sharpened the air! I was shaking.

The poor papa read a chapter from the Bible. He described his loving son's life, in doleful honourableness.

"There are a thousand flowers in Spring,"—the poet spoke—"whose repute is not extensively spoken, like that of the rose or violet. Some of them are not given even a name. They spend their smile and odour into the breeze, and die without any repining. They are content, because they are true to God. So a poet's life

115

should be. What is celebrity? Keats was told of his beautiful graveyard, and he said: 'I have already seemed to feel the flowers growing over me.' If this poet, whom we now bury, had been told of this hill, he might have said: 'I see already the butterflies beaming over my head.' Spring is coming. The poppies and buttercups shall dress the hill."

A church-bell chimed from the valley.

We left the buried to his solitude.

My uncle and I sat under an acacia tree, silent for some time.

"Look, Morning Glory!" he said, exhibiting a silver piece.

"Is there any story about that dollar?"

"The father of the dead paid me for carrying the coffin."

"Uncle, did you accept it?"

"Yes."

"Such a funny uncle!"

"Why not?"

"You have spoiled all your nobility for only one dollar."

I upturned my face, afterward, appealing in gleeful tone:

"O Uncle, you ought to give me half of it. Fifty cents! I carried the bench, you know."

15th—I arose at the first whistling of a meadow-lark.

Hearken to its hailing morning voice!

O simple bird!

Its so various moods are expressed only in its eternally changeless syllables. What a magical song!

How bungling seemed our human vocabularies!

I trod the garden in bare feet.

Naked feet, sir!

The delicious chilliness of the ground animated me rapturously. Do you believe me if I confess that I knelt and kissed it? I said that I would not mind burying my nude body for a few hours. Mother earth is so sweet.

I ran up the hill, humming an Oriental ditty.

The air was relishable, like an ice-cream on a summer midnight.

The beautiful sun was rising.

I clapped my palms thrice, reverently bowing.

Am I a sun-worshipper?

Yes!

I cleansed my feet in the water of the creek when I returned from the hill. I sat me on a rock, extending my bare feet in the sunlight. I thought that towel-wiping was too much of a modernism.

"Uncle! O Uncle!" I called.

"What is it, Miss Morning Glory?"

The poet jutted out from a bamboo bush by the wooden bridge over the creek.

"Such charming feet!" he said.

I instantly lowered my skirt, blushing.

He was carrying a spade and hoe. He said that he had been planting flowers about the grave of our friend, ever since four o'clock. "To make it beautiful is high poetry," he philosophised.

"What do you wish with Uncle, my child?" he continued.

"I want my shoes."

"Let me have the honour of fetching them for you!" he said in amiably dignified docility.

16th—The poet gave me five feet square, behind the Willow Cottage, for my potato garden.

I sticked a stick at each corner. I encircled it with my crape sash.

The note hanging on it read, "Graveyard of Morning Glory's Poem."

I hired uncle for ten cents, to clear off every weed.

I raked.

I set the seeds.

I got a suspicious coat and pants from a nook in the unrespectable barn. It was fortunate that the horse—who may also be a poet, he is so philosophically thin,—didn't shout, "Hoa, clothes-thief!"

I put them on the limbs of an acacia tree.

I planted it on my graveyard to scare away wild intruders.

It is holy ground.

I wondered when the potatoes would grow.

17th—Squirrel!

What admirable eyes!

He projected his head from a hole by my window. He withdrew it a bit, and bent it to one side, as if he were solving a question or two.

Then his eyes stabbed my face.

"I'm no questionable character, Mr. Squirrel," I said.

He hid himself altogether.

I amassed some crusts of bread by his hole, and watched humbly for his honourable presence.

He did not peep out at all.

The bread was not a worthy invitation. I varied it with a fragment of ham.

Mr. Squirrel wasn't void-stomached.

I thought he needed something to read. I tore a poem from the wall. I left it by his respectable cavern.

Lo!

His head sprouted out to pull it in.

"Aha, even the squirrel is a poetry devotee, in this hill!" I said in humourous mood.

18th—

"Most Beloved:

"Mamma was flogged with a bamboo rod some hundred times when she was a girl, her exchanging of a word with a boy over the fence being deemed an obscenity. My papa spent his lonely days in a room with Confucious till one night a middleman left him with my mamma as with a dolly. I do believe they never wrote any love letter.

"What would they say, I wonder, if they knew that

118

their daughter had taken to Love-Letter Writing as a profession in Amerikey?

"You shouldn't censure my penury in writing, knowing that I am a musume from such a source.

"Oscar, are your windows clean?

"Every window of my Willow Cottage was washed yesterday. Is there anything more happy to see (your beautiful eyes excepted) than a shiny window? I pressed my cheek to the window mirthfully, when Mr. Poet tried to pinch it from the outside. My dearest, if he had been my very Mr. Ellis!

"I made a discovery while I was trimming about the kitchen.

"Can you guess what it was?

"'Love-Letter Writer!'

"'Gift from Heaven!' I said, trusting it would help me in my composition.

"I lit a candle last night. I hid it behind the cover of such a huge bible which I had borrowed for the purpose. I was heedful of two old men who might disturb me, mistaking the light for a sign that something had happened. Poor Mrs. Heine almost cried, she was so pleased to think that I loved the Bible. Do I love it? Oho, ho, ho——

"Bakabakashi, how sad!

"The whole bunch of letters wasn't fit for my taste at all, at all.

"I'm sorry that I used up two candles that were all we had in this hill.

"So, my darling, my letter has to be woven from my truest heart.

"Good morning, my sweet lord! How are you? Have you breakfasted? Did you eat a beefsteak? I dislike a hearty morning eater. My ideal man shouldn't be given more than a cup of coffee and one trembling leaf of bacon.

"Mr. Poet kills a frog every morning. He says that his

fancy springs like a pond singer when he tastes it. I should say that his idea bounds too far in his case.

"Do you eat frog?

"I beseech you not to incline toward it.

"What should I do if your thought ran off from me?

"Failure of my life! Love is the whole business of woman, you know.

"Have you any shirt to mend?

"I have been fixing the poet's.

"Pray, express it to me!

"Should you ask such a pleasure of any other girl, it would be a fatal mistake for you. Remember, Oscar, that the Japanese girl is a mightily jealous thing!

"My sweetheart, I dreamed a dream.

"You were a dragonfly, while I was a butterfly. It is needless to say that we loved. One spring day we floated down along the canyon from a mountain a thousand miles afar. Our path was suddenly barred by a dense bush. We couldn't attain to the Garden of Life without adventuring in it. So, then, you stole in from one place, I from another. Alas! We got parted forever.

"Isn't that a terrible indication?

"Do you know any spell to turn it good? I am awfully agitated by it.

"Oh, kiss!

"Kiss me, my dear!

"I have to ascertain your love in it.

"Your
"Morning Glory"

19th—A little "chui chui" was building a nest under the roof, by my door.

Dear jovial toiler!

I must help him in some way.

I unravelled one of my stockings, hoping it might be serviceable in bettering his home.

I stood me on a chair, raising up my arms with my gift.

The poor sparrow was scared. He cast a gray "honourableness" on my hand.

O naughty "chui chui!"

He winged away, twittering, "chui, chui, chui!"

20th—The squirrel by my window shows a great fancy for me. He honoured me three times already this morning. He bore a somewhat scholarly air. A retired professor, I reckon.

Is he regular with his diary?

Possibly he is idle with a pen, like any other professor.

Let me scribble for him to-day!

My one bottle of ink has some time to dry up yet.

I will name it "The Cave Journal." I will leave it to the Professor for a souvenir upon my sayonara to this hill.

A

Where are my spectacles?

B

Upon my soul, I believe that some mischief is raging. I can never trust even the poet abode. Who stole my two-cent stamp?

God bless you, my precious daughter at Sierra Nevada!

By and by I will erect my private telegraph between us.

C

The idea of an idiotic spider tying his net across my front gate!

How ever could he be so ambitious as even to incline to arrest me!

He may very likely be a detective. A railroad brigand is hiding in these Heights, I suppose.

The world is running worse every day.

How shocking!

It was a fundamental error of God, to create that adventuress Eve. The offspring of a crow can't be other than a crow.

121

Our squirrel history is not blotted by any criminal. I feel a bit conceited in speaking about it. How can I help it?

The trouble with God is that he was awfully vain to express his own ability by so many useless things.

Rifle, for instance.

My poor wife!

D

To-day is the anniversary of my beloved. She was shot by one two-legged barbarian.

I appealed to the police. American police are rotten, through and through. The murderer bribed them, I fancy.

I found my wife, but she was only a skin.

How often did I tell her that she was risking too much in sporting around! But she didn't mind me, insisting that sight-seeing was a better education.

I carried her skin into my home.

I cleansed it, and altered its form a trifle, because it was a lady's. I am still keeping it for church-wear.

I feel dreadful, thinking of her.

E

A butterfly passed by my cavern, a hundred times.

Each time she threw me a vulgar laugh.

Her face was thickly powdered in yellow. Does she think herself charming? I should say that I would prefer a girl in tights from a saloon-stage to her indecency.

Such a flirt!

I suppose that she wanted me to marry her.

No!

Am I not old enough to avoid running into such foolishness?

F

Rainy day!

I sat in a memorial corner of my cave, with an unfinished novel of my wife's.

I do judge she had flashes of genius. She was so deep, like the sky. I never suspected that she could gracefully have beaten George Eliot, if she had only survived.

Poor girl!

One tenderly loved by God passes away young.

I have fallen into the habit of crying unmanfully nowadays.

I cannot help it, can I?

G

One thing I must furnish is a bathroom.

Cleanliness is the first rule of heaven, I am told.

I went to the lily pond to take a gracious bath.

O such water gamins! Dirty-handed frogs!

How could I dip me in the turbid water?

The frogs ought to go to a reformatory school. They have no culture, whatever.

H

Camera hunters are thick as fogs.

To-day I came near being a victim.

No, sir!

I can't permit my picture to be seen with those of cheap matinee idols. I must keep some dignity.

Americans are too commercial altogether. The pictures of our race are in demand, I imagine.

I

Beautiful moon, last night!

I filled my stomach with the divine water from a creek.

My face waved in the water. I flattered myself that I was a pretty handsome gentleman.

I sang an ancient Chinese song:

"Come 'long, to-morrow moon,
Carrying a harp!"

J

Stop your empty noise, meadow-larks!

Silence is the first study of this hill and the last, don't you know?

I am absorbed in my grave work, "The Secret of the World."

K

My neighbouring Jap girl is rather attractive, isn't she?

I heard a few scratches of her native bubbling.

The pagan speech is not so bad as I thought.

L

If there is one thing I cannot endure, it is ignorance.

What is the state of your roses, old boy?

The poet Heine is utterly alien to rose culture. Shall I order "How to Raise Roses" from a London publisher?

M

I went up the hill to pray to God. The higher the nearer.

When I came back, my honourable vestibule was blocked, I found, by the dirt. The poet was ditching close by my residence.

I couldn't blame his conduct, however, because no one could see my home. I don't hang out a sign like a quack doctor.

It occurred to me that I would strike into his cottage, and snatch the best poems from his drawer, and sell them with my name.

"I must secure the international copyright," I said.

But I couldn't dare it, my impulse being thwarted.

I am no wicked reporter, don't you see?
I hid me in his historical iron pot all day.

N

Heine was posting around the following card:

No Shooting.

I venture to say that he is the only one civilised Two-Legged in the whole world.

O

Where is my napkin?
Chinese laundry isn't punctual in delivery.

P

I think I must learn how to swear for a pastime.

Q

My fellow brother Mr. — — was shot this morning.

The paper says that there is a possibility of war between Russia and Japan. A preacher prophesies the disappearance of the universe.

Everything is precarious in the extreme.

I will not poke around outside during the day. I will loaf in the poet's orchard under the breezy moonlight.

Poetical existence is just enough. I will withdraw me to the sanctuary of the Muses.

R

Heaven be with my soul! Amen!

Good-bye, my dear old world!

21st—A Chinaman passed with a weighty load of washing on his shoulder.

"Friend, stop a minute! Take a glass with me before you go!"

The poet rolled out with a claret bottle.

Did you ever see a Chinee in love? Did you ever see one smile?

Mr. Charley smiled a serene smile of the Flower Kingdom pattern.

"God bless the Empress Dowager!" Mr. Poet said. Both raised their wine.

"The load is too heavy for you. You are killing yourself. I can't bear to see it. My friend, obey me! Let me help you! Don't leave till I come back!"

The poet, hurried for his questionable buggy and horse. He cracked his whip—he never whips the horse, but he carries it for fashion's sake, as he remarks—when Mr. Charley protested, "Me oll-righ, you savvy!"

The Chinaman was dumbfounded, for the poet was unknown to him.

Mr. Heine pushed him in.

When he leaped up, he noticed his horse in tender tone:

"Go on, baby!"

"What a goody-goody! His act never parts from poetry, however," I said.

I was simply dying for an opportunity to explode my good heart, when I invited one tramp to my Willow Cottage.

I fed him with one dozen eggs.

I emptied out all my change for him.

"Don't you feel cold, lying outdoors?" I said.

"Yes, Miss!"

"Don't you need an overcoat?"

"Yes, Miss!"

When Mr. Tramp left me with an overcoat in his hand, looking like a proud Mayor of Tokio, my uncle was coming from Mrs. Heine's.

"Uncle, you do want to be good to a poor man, don't you? You have made yourself a great philanthropist with your overcoat."

"What have you done?"

"I presented it to a tramp."

"Morning Glory!"

"Never mind, Uncle! I will buy a swell coat in New York. You have some more, haven't you?"

"It cost me forty yens at 'Hama. You really are a foolish girl, Asagao!"

(Asagao is my humble name in Japanese.)

Then I kissed his hand most pathetically—in fun for my part, of course.

22nd—My superstitious Mamma!

She mailed me an o mikuji from the holy box of the Akiwa god.

The number written on the slip was fifty-one. The divine will read as follows:

"Faith in the Well-God will result fortunately."

Mamma bade me make my prayer long (not mixing it with any laughter whatever).

I wondered whether there was any well around here.

I explored. I came across one (such a doubtful well) by an apple tree.

I hastened to my cottage to cut a paper flag.

The poet gave me one cup of claret for the Well-God.

I sat by the well.

What did I pray?

I pried into the well for the fin of a fish. Well without a funa fish isn't holy to a Jap mind.

23rd—Uncle left the Heights for Frisco.

I have encountered somewhere one picture, "Stolen Kiss," symbolising sweetness.

I dare say the sweetest thing in the world is to steal into a gentleman's room and over-turn his things.

The gentleman smell is provocative.

My uncle?

I can only say that he is more desirable than an old woman. Old woman is sad as a dry persimmon.

I stole into his room.

God will overlook my petty crime—how lovely to be scratched by guilt!—in consideration of the fact that a Jap girl never profanes.

I turned his pillow. Pillow is a fascination for me ever since I have read of a poet who hid his diary under it.

Look at the book, "A Random Note!"

He was working to beat me with his journal, I derided.

I sat on his bed, opening it.

"How original!" I exclaimed.

Uncle, you are a cynic, aren't you?

Let me pick a few pieces from his pen!

"Unfortunately! Japanese are accustomed from babyhood to depend on another's back. The hereditary fashion of nursing the baby on the back has thoroughly taught them dependence. Independence is only a coat of arms to distinguish man from the beasts—that is all. I urge that Emerson's essays be adopted in the Nippon schools. His 'Self-reliance' should be the first of all.

"Most unhappily! I have observed the Japanese fad in America for years, and it has not yet reached its culmination. Each month the books on Japan are placed before the public. It is verily sad even to cut their edges. (The practical Americans prove themselves unpractical in leaving the leaves of books uncut.) I say that our Japan is entitled to regard for worthier things than geisha girls or a fashion in bowing. We should decline your love, Americans, if it is rooted merely in your fancy for our paper lanterns. I have frequently come to conclude that Americans are eminently the freakish nation. I feel not only occasionally that they lack the reasoning power. I do not assume the phenomena of the yellow journals as my proof.

"A year or two ago, one Japanese theatrical troup roamed. They are not catalogued at home as actors. They chose to skip on the stage, simply because a bit more money is in it than in the calling of 'lantern-carrying for politicians.' Any wild animal can skip. I am now confronted with the question whether American generosity is not without sense. They piled up their money for them. Even the first-class critics struggled to find out something from such poor art. I am bound to be thankful, however, for the Americans saved these poor players from bankruptcy in Japan. It reminds me of a story. Our Nippon government many years ago appointed a certain loafing sailor as an English instructor, giving him a monthly pay of three hundred dollars. Sailor with an anchor-tatoo on his hand! Three hundred dollars are no small coin in Japan. Our sailor professor said, I am told, that he had not heard of any Milton. Ignorance can easily be a philanthropist, if it can be anything.

"Japanese love Nature? They do. But how sad to glance at Japanese garden! It is painful to notice the dwarf trees. Japs never permit one thing to grow naturally. Country of deformity! America, most natural, most manly nation!"

24th—My uncle didn't come back yesterday. Mr. Poet condescended to the town.

I am alone.

I spent the entire forenoon with Grandma, peeling potatoes, strewing sweet pea seeds on the ground.

I ascended the hill with the root of a white rose—believing in the Nippon idea that blossoms for the dead should be white—and set it by the grave.

Then I stole into the canyon.

I amassed the dead leaves of redwood by the brook for a camp-fire.

The smoke rose like a soul unto heaven.

I watched its beautiful confusion.

When I left, a snake obstructed my path, flashing its needle of a tongue.

Snake, one of my greatest foes! (The others being cheese and mathematics.)

I turned pale.

But I bravely faced it, hoping that it would speak a word or two, as one did to Eve. I placed my eyes on it, though in fear. Perhaps it wasn't as intelligent as the one in the garden of Eden. Maybe it thought it nothing but a waste of time to address a Jap poorly stored in English. It crept away.

I ran down the hill.

A storm of laughter struck me from within when I came to my Willow Cottage. I examined it from the window. Half a dozen young ladies were biting pie. (Pie! Rustic pastry I ever so hate!)

"Picnic!" I murmured.

My blood gushed up. I was on the verge of denouncing their irruption. The cottage belongs to any one, I said in my afterthought, as it does to me.

I slipped away.

I found myself in the plum orchard with a hoe.

I began to root the weeds. I waited silently for their departure.

25th—The spring hills were coquetting like a tea-house maiden, singing:

> "The air is lovely like wine;
> Come, Lord! Come, Lord!"

The curtain for the spring comedy has not yet risen.

Already the picnic band invades.

To-day I will make myself mistress of a hillside coffee-house.

The poet—the eternally sweet poet—hastened to borrow a tent from a neighbour.

He set it on the greenest spot of grass before my cottage. I must excuse his conceit, he entreated, in showing his skill by baking a cake for me.

"Accept my hundred arigatos!"

I bowed demonstratively.

I pasted a paper—such a bashful brown piece from a butcher's table—with the sign of

"BISHOPS' REST"

The poet tacked "Ten Cents for Coffee and Cake" on the fence by the tent.

The cups (what a shame that their arms were all off) were rinsed, when he showed me an imperial poundcake, declaring it his own manufacture.

At three o'clock I was fully prepared for an honorable guest.

The coffee on the oil-stove was surging, when two parties went by, not spending even one look at my sign.

"Times are awfully hard, I think. People have not luxury enough to spare even a dime," I murmured sadly.

I said that I would have no business, if I didn't make the next party my victim.

I appeared before the tent, when a few girls—who were born for laughing, but not for thinking—came close by.

"Will you rest and taste the cake that the poet made, ladies?" I said.

"That's nice," they said, rolling into the tent.

I served them with coffee and cake.

"Is this surely the poet's cake? It looks like baker's cake," one girl said.

"Mr. Poet assured me it was of his own making," I replied in cool reserve.

After they left, I scrutinised the cake. Oya! A little bakery mark was seen.

"Mighty liar!" I grumbled.

Abrupt clouds clouded the sun. The winds scolded bitterly. I decided there was no business remaining.

I called Mr. Heine and uncle into the Bishops' Rest.

"Your cake was fine, Mr. Poet."

"I know it, Miss Morning Glory. I'm a pretty good cook, you see. I cooked once in a Sierra camp for fifty miners. I was paid twenty dollars a week. Alas! It was the biggest money I ever earned."

"By the way, Mr. Heine, the bakery sent a bill for you."

I placed before him a slip that I had prepared for the purpose.

"Ha! Ha, ha, ha!"

131

His open laughter was as from a simple Faun.

I noticed, afterward, a black mass heaped in a ditch. The whole situation grew plain to me. He couldn't bake, but only burn, in the oven, and had despatched his neighbour for the cake.

Dear Poet!

26th—We pressed the poet to receive some money as just a sign of our gratitude.

Mr. Heine despised our thought.

Honourable gentleman!

I found a tin box. I put the money in—ask me not how much!

I dug a hole by the willow tree beside the lily pond, and buried the money box. I tumbled a stone over it to mark it.

"I'll write him about it from New York. See, Uncle! Isn't it unique?" I said.

Uncle wasn't enthusiastic in approving my idea. He couldn't check me, however, as the money was mine.

He said he would order an elegant vase from Tokio.

27th—I intended to keep a sweet fashion of old Japan in presenting a poem at my sayonara.

We will take leave to-morrow.

O gracious graceful poet abode!

My farewell poem in seventeen syllable form is as follows:

"Sayonara no
Ureiya nokore
Mizu no neni!"

"Remain, oh, remain,
My grief of sayonara,
There in water sound!"

28th—Mrs. Heine kissed me.

Dear old Grandma!

"Do you know what this is, Miss Morning Glory?" the poet said, plucking a leaf from a tree by his door.

"Fig-leaf! Isn't it?"

"Yes, my child! It is a fig-leaf. Do you know the fig tree? It is the shyest tree in the world. Classical tree, indeed! It has no blossom, being so modest of display, but it has the fruits. Remember, my young lady, its teaching of 'Modesty! Modesty!'"

"Sayonara, Mr. Poet!"

"One minute, Uncle!" I said.

I ran into the Willow Cottage to get a cupful of water. I watered my friend Miss Poppy with love.

Bye-bye, little girl!

San Francisco, March 1st

Civilisation again!

The first thing was to buy a cake of the best soap.

Because my hands had perfected their transformation into worthless leather while I dwelt on the hill.

What kind of soap did I use, do you suppose?

Laundry soap.

2nd—Delightful Ada!

We drove to the Cliff House, Ada to laugh at the stupid song of the seals, I to say my adieu.

Good-bye, Pacific Ocean!

We cried in hugging.

We shall not see each other for some time,—maybe never again!

Ada!

O Ada San!

3rd—This afternoon!

Eastward, ho, ho!

Overland Train, March 4th

"Madame Butterfly" lay by me, appealing to be read.

"No, iya, I'll never open! I erred in buying you," I said.

I dislike that "Madame." It sounds indecent ever since the "gentleman" Loti spoiled it with his "Madame Chrysanthème."

The honourable author of "Madame Butterfly" is Mr. Wrong. (Do you know that Japanese have no boundary between L and R?) Undoubtedly, he is qualified to be a Wrong.

Authorship is nothing at all, nowadays, since authors are thick as Chinese laundries.

Well, still, it can be honourable, if it is honourable.

Japanese fiction penned by the tojin!

It is a completely sad affair. I wonder why the author (God bless him) didn't fit himself for brooming the streets instead of scrawling.

The characters in his book—I am grateful I see no lady writer of Japanese novels yet—remind me of the "devils of mixture" swarming in Yokohama or Kobe, whose Jap mother was a professional "hell." It is lamentable to set the verdict on them that they have inherited the art of framing lies from their mamma.

Do I vex you, gentleman, when I say that your Japanese type could only be an unprincipled half-caste?

Your Nippon character eyed in blue, and hairy-skinned always. Isn't it absurd when it puts a 'Merican shoe on one foot and a wooden clog on the other?

And if you insist on registering it as a Jap, I shall merely laugh loudly.

One heroine I have read of placed a light summer haori over her heavily padded mid-winter clothes.

Your Oriental novel, let me be courageous enough to say, is a farce at its best.

Oh, just wait, my sweet Americans! A genuine one will soon be offered to you by Morning Glory.

I stepped out to the platform, and threw out "Madame Butterfly."

Poor "Madame!"

I trust in the mountain lions of high Nevada to cherish her lovingly.

5th—

"Matsuba Sama, the following letter creeps 'under your honourable table.'

"How is yourself?

"I imagine that the breeze fills your bower with the odour of ume flowers. I am definite in saying that the Japanese ume is of different origin from the California plum tree, which has no expression in divine fragrance as I am told. I see your indolent face in the air, awaiting poetical inspiration on your bamboo piazza where the ume petals are beautifully blotched.

"There are several months yet till we shall quarrel face-to-face over the superiority of English or Oriental literature.

"Miss Pine Leaf, I—or rather we—have said farewell to Frisco.

"It was sad that I never saw any battleship (excepting one shamefaced gunboat) in the bay of the Golden Gate. A bay without battleship is like a door without a lock.

"Can you fancy any Japanese city without soldiers?

"American soldier?

"I am sorry to say that I have met no soldier in my four months at the Pacific.

"I presume that the practical Meriken jins can't bear to see such a useless ornamentation. Yes! Soldiers are degenerating, in my opinion, to the rank of a fireplace on a hot summer day. How stimulating, however, was the sound of the fearless hoofs of a cavalier! When the sabres of a regiment flashed in the sunlight, I could never keep from fluttering my paper handkerchief.

"I shall not excite myself in such a joy in Amerikey.

"I made the acquaintance of one colonel at Mrs. Willis'. He is a jolly business man. Just think of a colonel plus merchant! Is it possible? He changes his white shirt every morning, and shines his shoes twice a day. I should say that he will carry a sheet and opera hat, and leave his gun behind, whenever he is summoned to a battle-field. Possibly he has hidden his colonelship in his trunk.

135

"I found afterward that every old gentleman is a colonel or judge.

"Everything in California is made for just a woman.

"California gentleman isn't privileged to raise one question against a lady. He is provided with all sorts of exclamations to please the woman. If he should ever miss one dinner with his wife, he would be divorced in court on the morrow.

"Uncle says that the Eastern gents are not so devoted to the lady.

"If it be true!

"Am I now entering the city of Man?

"How sad!

"Have you any experience of writing by the car-window?

"I feel a strange delight in scanning my romantically tremulous handwriting. A certain famous Jap penman takes wine before he begins, for the sake of putting his mind in a fine frenzy, as you know. The shaking of the car produces in me the same effect. Isn't this letter great enough to be honoured on your tokonama?

"Can you ever imagine how vast Amerikey is?

"Yesterday our car ran all day long, over the mountains and prairies, seeing only a few huts.

"O such a snowstorm in the evening!

"The train rushed like a maddened dragon. It was verily an astonishingly ghastly spectacle as any human thought could ever picture. I thrilled with a feeling of tragic ecstasy, which is the highest emotion.

"Can you recollect that you and I once stood under the darkest rains without an umbrella, and laughed hysterically?

"I love shocking emotion.

"Since I was touched by the continental air, I measure my lungs dilating two inches bigger. How sorry I shall be for you when I return! You are so tiny! I expect myself to be five inches higher within the next few months.

136

"Amerikey is the country where everything grows, don't you know?

"Even the stars look a deal larger than in Japan.

"Looking back at the Rocky Mountains,

"*Yours,*
"*Asagao*"

6th—The rocking of the train makes us babies in the cradle.

The car is a modern opium resort, where we sleep and sleep.

I shouldn't wonder if we all turned into nodding Rip Van Winkles.

To-day I had a sleeping contest with uncle.

I was defeated.

Chicago, 7th

Chicago water is a perfect horror.

Gomenyo! That's no way to begin, is it?

I never waver in saying that California girls borrow their fairness from their water.

There is no question in my mind why the Chicago women—certain hundreds I saw, if you please—are barren in their complexion.

"O Uncle, how many days have we to tarry here?" I asked, within an hour after we had set foot in this city.

I grieve over my contact with such a city. It is no place for a lady. (Is here any lady?) It is just the place for a man.

No show marked "Only for a Man" is respectable, I dare say.

Are Chicago men "gentlemen?"

They are not sensitive about their hats in the hotel elevator. The laundry work isn't superb, I judge, as not every one's shirt is snowy as a San Franciscan's. I cannot blame their black finger-nails, as they live in smoke.

Even the Frisco smoke hindered my breath at my opening moment in Amerikey. I should have died, if it had been Chicago.

137

Bodily cleanliness is the first chapter in the whitening of the soul. How many mortals are there here with a clear soul?

"Chicago is Mr. Nobody without the smoke, like Japan without a fan. The prosperity of a modern city is measured by the bulk of its smoke, Morning Glory. But I don't approve of their using a cheap coal. Health has to be guarded," my uncle said.

A driver carried us from the station as if we were pigs.

Mind you, this is Chicago illustrious for its hams.

I barred my ears with my hands in the carriage. The thunderous noise menaced me so.

Do roses blossom well in the turbulent air?

I have no doubt that Chicago has no poet.

"Cook County fosters three thousand poets, one paper says, my young woman," Uncle said in laughter.

"Don't say so!"

"As soon as I had established myself in the hotel, I inscribed— with the longest apologetical ojigi to Mr. Shelley—as follows:

> "Hell is a city much like Chicago,
> A populous and a smoky city."

8th—How sad I felt, not to be greeted by even one star from my hotel window last night!

I was disgusted with the poor taste of the coffee. Such a first-class hotel! Coffee and maxim, I have said, should be of the very best. Commonplace words with the golden heading of Maxim would be as cheap as a negress with white powder. I would choose even a bread pudding rather than a suspicious cup of coffee.

Uncle failed to secure a box of cigarettes.

The most delicate shape for smoking is the slender stalk of a cigarette. The cigar ever so much impresses me as barbarous. Chicagoans might say it was the only manly smoke.

Truly!

Chicago is the City of Man (whatever that means).

I'm glad that the young gentlemen with genteel canes under their arms don't open any cigar-stand conference here. Such an abomination in Frisco!

No drones, whatever.

My uncle was going out sight-seeing with me in a silk hat.

I objected to it.

Plug hat doesn't suit informal Chicago.

He changed his frock-coat for a sack-coat.

"Now, Uncle, you look more like a Chicago gentleman!" I said.

Yes, this is a plain sack-coat city.

He was fussing with a handkerchief. I said, laughing: "Never mind, Uncle! I am sure the men don't carry it here, since the women never carry a purse in their hand."

Isn't it awful that one (even a stranger) ought to know everything in Chicago? A slight question to the street people would be condemned as a nuisance.

Even the policeman shows no chivalry.

I was sorry that the colour of his suit was bitterly faded.

Isn't Chicago rich enough to furnish a new one?

I suppose many dogs must be hanging around here, because the policeman arms himself with a piece of wood for chasing them off.

I should like to know if there is any blacker house than the City Hall.

It will be a matter of a short time before the Chicago River turns to ink.

Then we went to observe the Lake of Michigan from Lincoln Park.

I scoffed at my absurdity in being ready with the first line for my poem on the lake. If you knew that "O minstrel of Heaven and Truth!" was the beginning, you would laugh surely. The lake wasn't a huge singer like the Pacific Ocean, at all.

"Uncle, please, count how many stories in that building!" I begged.

Chicago structures "crush my little liver" completely. Did I ever dream that I would eye such pillars of the sky in my life?

When I returned to my hotel, I declared that I would not open my trunk, because my everyday dress was good enough for Chicago.

I regret to say that the gentlemen are so homely.

9th—How dear is the green crispy paper money.

What a historical look!

It made me feel as if I were at home.

I hated ever so much the gold coin in California. Its threateningly mercantile aspect made me shudder as at a speculator of Kakigara Cho of Tokio.

If I like Chicago it must be on account of its soiled paper money.

I will exchange all my gold to it.

I went to one store for a short skirt like that Chicago woman wears.

It may be a change, though shortness in hair and dress is my aversion. It may be advantageous in showing one's shoes, though eternal exhibition isn't tasty.

It would be an accurate account of my reason for buying to say that I singularly wished to use up a few jumbles of money.

I dulled myself reading the advertising bills through my hotel window.

There's no block free from them.

'Vertisement!

Isn't it horrid?

I laughed, wondering why those enterprising Meriken jins don't employ the extensive backs of prizefighters in the ring.

Uncle and I went to see the Injuns dance.

How fantastically they sang!

There was a Japanese tea-house.

It is no "tea-house" at all. It was the saddest thing I ever saw.

I thought that Chicagoans were not fastidious with anything.

"Any old thing will do!" they might say jollily.

Open, hard-working Chicago!

Has she much education?

10th—My uncle wanted me to join him in visiting a stockyard to see the doomed pigs groaning, "Fu, fu, fu!"

I declined.

Uncle started off alone.

There was some time before I heard someone fisting on my door.

"A Japanese gentleman wishes to see your husband, madam," a hotel attendant addressed me.

"Good God! My husband?" I cried.

Satemo!

How could any porter be such an ignoramus as not to distinguish between Mrs. and Miss!

Possibly he esteemed me "modern" enough to marry an old man for money's sake.

Oya, he was Mr. Consul of Chicago.

"Walk in, sir! Uchino hito will return within an hour or so."

Then I explained about "my husband."

We both laughed.

There is nothing more pleasing when in an alien country than a chit-chat in our native "becha becha."

Japanese speech!

Such a beautifully indefinite, poetically untidy language!

I love it.

11th—It would be too much of a risk of one's life to stay in Chicago.

Good-bye!

Flowerless, birdless city, sayonara!

Buffalo, 12th

Niagara Falls was a disappointment.

Uncle says I have still to learn how to be appreciative of things.

A red brick chimney by the Fall spoils the whole affair, I do think.

My uncle was cross, saying that he had eaten the toughest beef of his life.

He seized two Canadian dimes and a bogus half-dollar in an hour.

"Poor Uncle! Isn't this Buffalo town awful?" I said.

141

New York, 13th

Miss Morning Glory has stepped into Greater New York, at last.

Thirteenth of March, 1900.

To-day will be the special day of my family history.

My entrance was delightful to the full.

The train stole gracefully into the city at early morn. The sky was distinct like the lake of Biwa. The respectable face of the city accepted us charmingly.

I bounced my little body in my happy thought of another chapter of life.

I felt like Dante crawled out of darkest Hell, after the torture of the terrible show. (O Chicago!)

Our kind Japanese consul of New York was looking after our arrival with a carriage.

I saw a horse-car trotting.

It encouraged me to think that even an ignorant Jap girl might find her own living here, since such an old-fashioned thing exists perfectly.

I secretly fixed in my mind that I will adventure my independent life when the crisis demands.

Our carriage rolled up Fifth Avenue to Central Park.

How often had I imagined laying me in this celebrated ground!

"Pray, let me off to smell the smell of the New York breeze!" I exclaimed.

When I was stationed on the third floor of an edifice on Riverside Drive—what a brisk name in the world!—which was Mr. Consul's home, my bubbling fancies hastened down with the waters of the Hudson River under my window.

Hudson River?

It is my dear old acquaintance, introduced by the ever so pleasing Mr. Irving.

See its classical profundity before my face!

Where's "Sleepy Hollow," I wonder!

The spectacle of the river reminded me of the Sumida Gawa of Tokio, mirroring the clouds of affectionate cherry blossoms which border its bank. It would be a remarkable idea, I thought, to petition the Mayor of New York for the Japanese cherry-trees to parade on this side of the Hudson. When they are in flower, I will open a tea-house under them, of course. My attire as a mistress should be a little red crape apron to begin with. My head will be wound with a Japanese towel to endow my Oriental eyes with certain better results. I will raise my voice, calling, "Honourable rest! Honourable tea plucked by the choicest musumes!" What a novel!

Romance!

How can I live without it!

In that case I must entreat the removal of the characters on the other side, which are:

"Lots For Sale!"

Because I don't see any such unaristocratic sign by the Sumida Gawa.

14th—O snow, yukiya fure, fure!

The season of the city is still within the fence of winter. I was grateful to my fate that conveyed me here to overtake my loving snow.

I settled me by my window in absorption with the snow view of Hudson Gawa.

How busily the snowflakes fall!

Their cautiously silent hurry made me recollect the drama of the China-Japan war. How stealthily the soldiers marched at midnight! Can I ever forget how I tugged my shoji, crying "Victory, Dai Nippon!"

I raised the window, stretching out my arm. I collected the snow-petals in the hollow of my palm. I tasted them.

"Uncle, New York snow is as deliciously savoured as at home," I said.

Central Park must have been artistically attired.

"Oji San, let us go to the park for snow-viewing! I advise you to till a bit more poetry in yourself, Uncle," I announced.

I began to change my dress before his decision.

143

15th—We went to the famous Brooklyn Bridge.

Verily, New York gentlemen are interested with their papers in the car. Newspapers, O newspapers! There's no slip of a doubt that they would die without the sight of their newspapers. The unheroic part about them is that they forget neatly to offer their seats to a lady. Woman loves an absent-minded man once in a while, but never on the car, I do say.

I suppose every woman of this city has to be rich.

Must I equip a carriage?

I do not see why I could not win the first prize with my Louisiana ticket.

How I wish to fabric an every-inch-a-Japanese mansion on Fifth Avenue, and welcome a thousand tojins to hear my Jap song on Sunday!

"Is this bridge built for Americans or Europeans, Uncle? People crossing here use no English," I said.

"Liberty Statue!"

I will let the Beauty statue hail from the Bay of Yedo, when I am wealthy enough to afford it.

Doesn't Nippon signify beauty?

"How dear is that sign, 'Beware of Pick-pockets!' It makes me just feel as if I were at Shinbashi station in Tokio, doesn't it you, Uncle?"

Humbly humble 'rikisha men!

If I were besieged by them imploring me to take a little honourable ride, the scene would be complete.

I miss such a merry car in Amerikey.

We walked down Broadway. We came to a graveyard.

Tombstones in the midst of commerce!

O romantic New York!

I wondered how Wall Street gentlemen would be struck glancing at them.

What a soft silence hovered!

The old Gothic Church was my own ideal.

"Uncle, let us fall in and rest!" I cried.

The morning service was proceeding.

Alas and alas!

Not one soul was there.

Is this a religious city?

The inside was compact of heavenly purple air. Mr. Bishop—whatever he may be—gestured like another being from a loftier realm. A beautiful boy (there's no greater fascination than a boy with a prayer-book) supported the service. Intangibleness of speech is itself a divine charm.

"Will you mind asking Mr. Bishop whether he wants a sweeping girl? I wish I were given just a chance to clean such a holy church, uncle."

Then I looked up to Mr. Secretary.

16th—It seems to me a recent style that New York ladies discard their babies to leave them in the hands of European immigrants (very likely they want them to learn an ungrammatical hodge-podge, as respectableness is old-fashioned) and accompany a dog with mighty affection.

O my dear "chin" that I left at home!

Shall I call it to Amerikey?

Little loyal thing, pathetic, clinging!

I am sure it would beat any other in a dog contest.

17th—I never saw such hungry eyes in my life as those of an organ-grinder, set upon the windows for a dropping penny.

To an artist they would hint of a prisoner's bloodshot eyes numbed by useless gazing toward the light of the world.

Poor Italians!

They don't know one thing but turning the handle.

The last two days they placed their organ—read their sign, "Garibaldi & Co."—under my apartment at the same hour for my bit money.

I thought one of them might be a grandson of the renowned Italian patriot. How interesting it would be to be told of his shipwreck in life!

Now three o'clock.

There's one more hour before their frolic music will gush.

I must wrap some money in paper for them.

God bless them—simple creatures who work hard!

18th—Mr. Consul—an old man who sips the grayness of celibacy—never strays out from his official duty. He calls society and novels two recent pieces of foolery.

The family of Uncle's intimate is off in Europe.

The possibility of a nice time for me is verily illegible. Tsumaranai!

Last night I sketched an adventure of enlisting in the band of domestics.

"Capital idea to examine a New York household!" I said, when I left my breakfast table.

I humbled myself to a newspaper office with the following shamefaced advertisement:

"Jap girl, nineteen, good-looking, longs for a place in a family of the first rank."

I used every kind of oratory to bring my uncle to agree to my two weeks of freedom.

19th—Two letters were waiting me at the office.

One from No. 296 of a certain part.

296?

Unfortunately it sounds like "nikumu" in Japanese, meaning hatred.

And the other was from Fifth Avenue.

Parlour maid.

Twelve dollars for a month.

I shall accept it, since it is the proper quarter for seeing the high-toned New Yorker.

I feel already a servant feeling.

I am sorry that I didn't discipline myself before in dusting.

I will style me an honest worker for awhile. "Toiling for my daily bread," does ring an American sound, doesn't it?

"Domestic girl has no right, I think, to sit with Messrs. Consul and Secretary," I said, moving my dinner plate to the kitchen table.

Morning Glory, isn't it time you changed the book of your diary?

Really, sir!

Let me close now with a ceremonious bow!
My next book shall be entitled:
"The Diary of a Parlour Maid."

THE END